Lauris stood looking down at her

"Well, I'll say good-night, Julia. On Tuesday it will be, 'Good morning, Sister Mitchell.'"

"Like being two people," said Julia. "It's a pity—" She stopped and then went on, "Thank you for the lift. It was a nice weekend."

"Delightful. We hardly had a cross word."

He was staring at her and she studied his face carefully, suddenly wanting to learn every line of it. Not so young, perhaps, but still good looks to be reckoned with—indeed, he would never lose them, however old he was. When he wasn't being peppery he was one of the nicest people she had ever known.

That didn't include Nigel, of course, she added hastily to herself, she mustn't forget Nigel!

Books by Betty Neels

HARLEQUIN ROMANCE

These books may be available at your local bookseller.

Don't miss any of our special offers. Write to us at the following address for information on our newest releases.

Harlequin Reader Service
P.O. Box 52040, Phoenix, AZ 85072-2040
Canadian address: P.O. Box 2800, Postal Station A,
5170 Yonge St., Willowdale, Ont.   M2N 6J3

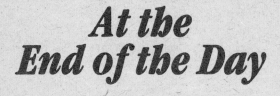

At the End of the Day

Betty Neels

Harlequin Books

TORONTO • NEW YORK • LONDON
AMSTERDAM • PARIS • SYDNEY • HAMBURG
STOCKHOLM • ATHENS • TOKYO • MILAN

Original hardcover edition published in 1985
by Mills & Boon Limited

ISBN 0-373-02729-X

Harlequin Romance first edition November 1985

CHAPTER ONE

UNDER an early morning September sky London was coming awake; the sun shone impartially on stately Regency houses, high rise flats and any number of parks. It shone too on St Anne's Hospital, a sprawling red brick edifice cramped by the mean streets around it, although not all were mean, in some of them the early Victorian houses, tall and narrow, each with its railed off area and attic windows, had made a brave effort to overcome shabbiness and were let out in flats or rooms. Even the attics had been converted into what were grandly called studio flats with tiny kitchens and showers squeezed into corners under the rafters.

The windows of one such flat, half way down a terrace in a side street lined with dusty plane trees, were open wide now, allowing the sun to shine in. It shone on the woman sitting in front of a rather battered dressing table, allowing her to take excellent stock of her reflection in its mirror. It was a charming one, although its owner didn't appear to like it overmuch. She had her hand up to her hair, tugging it this way and that, peering at it intently.

'There are bound to be some,' the woman said loudly and with impatience, 'I dare say the light's all wrong.' She abandoned her search and scrutinised her face, looking for wrinkles. But there weren't any of those either; her reflection frowned back at her, a lovely face with a creamy skin to go with her fiery hair and large green eyes. 'Well, there ought to be,' said the woman, 'the first grey hairs and wrinkles show up at thirty,' she added gloomily, 'next year I'll be thirty-one . . .'

She left the dressing table and crossed the room to drink the rest of a mug of tea on the table at the other side. She was a tall woman with generous curves, and despite her thirty years, looked a great deal younger. She finished the tea and began to dress and presently, in her dark blue sister's uniform, sat down in front of the mirror again and did her face and brushed her thick bright hair into a chignon. She had wasted time looking for the wrinkles; and there was only time for another pot of tea and some toast before she went on duty. She made the divan bed along one wall while the kettle boiled and then sat down at the table to drink the brew and munch her toast, wasting no time. Ten minutes later, the breakfast things stacked tidily in the sink in the tiny kitchen she let herself out of her room and locked the door, then with her cape slung over one shoulder ran down the three flights of stairs to the front door. No one else was about yet in the quiet street but once at its end she turned into a wider thoroughfare, bustling with morning traffic and early morning workers. It was a shabby street, with tatty shops and run down houses, and it led straight past the hospital gates, a mere five minutes' walk. All the same the woman had cut it fine and hurried across the courtyard and in through the imposing entrance, pausing in the enormous, gloomy hall to peer into the head porter's little office.

'Morning George, any letters?'

George, it was said jokingly, was as old as the hospital. He licked the pencil he was holding and on his newspaper made a cross by the name of the horse he intended to back later on that day before he answered. 'Good morning, Sister Mitchell, nice post for you this morning, too. Got a birthday?'

'As a matter of fact, I have.' She beamed at him and took the handful of cards and letters, longing to open them at once, but they would have to wait until she had taken the night nurses' report. She made for the stairs, taking them two at a time since there was no one except George to see her.

There was though; standing at the top of the wide staircase was a very large man with wide shoulders and a distinguished air, much heightened by the elegance of his clothes. He had dark hair, greying at the temples, dark eyes with drooping lids, a formidable nose and a mouth which was firm to the point of grimness.

Sister Mitchell, not expecting anyone on the half landing, skidded to a brief halt. Her good morning was brisk and friendly; she had no time to dally, not that Professor van der Wagema ever dallied . . .

He glanced at the thin gold watch on his wrist. 'Late, Sister Mitchell?' His voice was bland and had a nasty edge to it. 'Don't let me keep you from completing your gallop.'

'Oh, I won't, sir,' she assured him cheerfully and raced up the right hand wing of the staircase, reflecting as she went that it was a great pity that he was such an irritable man; so good looking, at the top of his profession and possessed, so rumour had it, of far more wealth than he needed. That was all rumour had been able to discover about him though. His private life was a closed book to all but his closest colleagues at the hospital, and they weren't likely to tell. 'Why's he here, anyway?' she muttered. 'Eight o'clock in the morning . . .' She went through the swing doors of the Women's Medical and crossed the landing to her office.

Three girls were waiting for her, her senior staff nurse, Pat Down, a quiet sensible girl with a pleasant face, and the two night nurses, one tall and fair with a pretty face and her junior, a small mouselike girl; all three looked flushed and harassed.

Sister Mitchell sat herself down at her desk. 'Good morning. Have we had a case in during the night?' She smiled at them. 'You all look worn out and I passed Professor van der Wagema on the stairs.'

'He was sent for at half-past six, Sister, I'm to tell you that he will be back later in the morning.' The senior night nurse answered.

'Splendid, shall we have the report then?'

The night nurse looked disappointed; in common with any number of the nurses at St Anne's, she considered Professor van der Wagema the answer to any ambitious girl's prayer, he might no longer be young like their numerous men friends, but he was infinitely more handsome even if he had a bad temper and wasn't above reducing them to tears with his sarcasm during lectures. All the same, she began on the report obediently; Sister Mitchell in her own small way, could be just as unbending, besides everyone knew that she and the professor didn't like each other.

'Miss Thorpe,' began the night nurse, 'Raynaud's disease . . .'

There were twenty-four patients, the report took quite a few minutes before the new admission could be mentioned; Mrs Collins, admitted in a coma of unknown origin at four o'clock. Examined by the medical officer on duty and by the medical registrar. Since she didn't respond to treatment Professor van der Wagema was called, who diagnosed a suspected cerebral embolism. 'Nothing's back from the Path Lab yet.' She added nursing details and Sister Mitchell asked: 'Relatives? Anyone come in with her, Nurse?'

'No, Sister. She lives in a room in Belsize Street and works in a factory in Limehouse; she didn't go to work and someone went round to see why not. No one seemed to know anything about her, so they got a policeman to open the door and found her on the floor.'

Sister Mitchell nodded slowly. 'Poor soul, let's hope someone turns up. The police have the details?' Her generous mouth curved in a smile. 'Thanks, Nurse, off with you both then. You're both on together tonight? Who's with Mrs Collins, Pat?'

'Nurse Wells, Sister, the other three are clearing breakfast and starting on the B.P. round.'

'Then let's go and take a look.'

Sister didn't hurry down the ward; she never appeared to do so, but she always managed to be where she was wanted. She went calmly, wishing any of the patients that caught her eye a good morning, and slid behind the cubicle curtains. She wished Nurse Wells a pleasant good morning, asked a handful of pertinent questions and bent to look at Mrs Collins, a lady of middle years and extremely stout. She was still deeply unconscious and after a minute Sister turned away. 'Let me know if you see anything, Nurse,' she warned and went back to her office; the morning's work would go on as usual; the student nurses would have to come to the office while she read the report to them and Pat kept an eye on the ward, she would have to get on to the Path Lab and get the results of the blood sugar and blood urea tests; it was far too soon to get the lumbar puncture results. There was the post too and her morning round . . .

The student nurses filed in, and she spent ten minutes going over the report with them and then allotting ward duties. That done, she was free to go back into the ward, armed with the day's letters and start the routine she never varied. The patients counted on her slow progress from bed to bed, it gave them a chance to air their grievances, complain about sleepless nights, ask questions about their condition and enlist her help over knotty problems they couldn't solve from their beds. She came to the last bed; Mrs Winter, a diabetic who had never quite grasped what was wrong with her and therefore spent a good deal of time in hospital being stabilised. 'I bin awake since four o'clock, Sister,' she said, avid for news of the new patient. 'Proper poorly, isn't she? All them doctors and nurses and the professor here, without his breakfast, I dare say, poor man.'

Julia Mitchell looked surprised. She had never thought of the professor in that light and certainly she had never pitied him, although now that she came to think about it, she was sorry for him although she wasn't sure why.

She said now in a soothing voice: 'Oh, I shouldn't worry, Mrs Winter, I expect he's got a wife to look after him.' A poor down-trodden creature, probably, never saying boo to a goose let alone to the professor. 'Did you eat all your breakfast, Mrs Winter?'

'The 'am, Sister dear, but I couldn't stomach the bread . . .'

'Did you eat none of it, Mrs Winter?' Julia asked

calmly; whichever nurse had seen to the diabetic breakfasts would have to be spoken to.

'No, ducks.'

'Then I'm going to bring you two cream crackers and you're going to eat every crumb. Will you do that?'

'Anything to please yer, love,' said Mrs Winter obligingly.

Julia went to the kitchen, found the crackers, put two on a plate and bore them to the ward. She hadn't quite reached it when she heard the swing doors open and close behind her and turned her head to see who it was. Professor van der Wagema, unsmiling as usual—perhaps he hadn't had his breakfast after all; she had no idea where he lived, but even if it had been next door to St Anne's which she very much doubted, he wouldn't have had time. She waved the plate of biscuits at him. 'I'll be right back, sir, Mrs Winter must have these now—she didn't eat her bread.'

She disappeared through the ward door and when she returned found him standing in the middle of the landing, still frowning.

'Mrs Collins is still unconscious, I've just had a quick look. The Path Lab are sending up the results within the next half hour. Do you want Doctor Reed?'

Doctor Reed was the registrar; a nice quiet little man who loved his work. He had a very large wife and any number of small children. The fact reminded her that she was feeling sorry for the professor.

'Would you like a cup of coffee?' she offered, and she added persuasively, 'and a biscuit?'

'You are thinking "Feed the brute",' said the professor, surprisingly.

'No—no, of course not. Only night nurse said you

were here early this morning and you can't have had much time for breakfast.'

He looked down his domineering nose at her. 'I can see no reason for you to concern yourself about my meals, Sister Mitchell. If it is convenient to you, I should like to see Mrs Collins.'

She didn't feel sorry for him any more. With her head high, she swept down the ward. Never again, she promised herself silently, would she offer him refreshment of any sort; of course the obligatory cup of coffee after his twice weekly rounds would have to be given to him, but that hardly counted. She slipped behind the curtains, nodded to Nurse Wells to go, and took up her position on the other side of the bed from the professor.

He bent over his patient, examining her with great care and presently Doctor Reed joined him. 'Difficult to determine hemiplegia,' muttered the professor, 'but I'm pretty certain it's a cerebral thrombosis.' He straightened up and glanced at Sister Mitchell. 'Have you any news of Mrs Collins' family or friends, Sister?'

'None,' said Julia, 'I've 'phoned the police and they've drawn a blank so far.'

'We must hope that they will have success before very long, it would be of considerable help to us. Now, as to treatment . . .' The professor never hummed and haa'd, he knew what he wanted done and made his wishes known concisely; what was more, he didn't like having to repeat his instructions, something Julia had discovered more than three years ago when she had taken over the ward. She had a good memory and was familiar with his ways; she listened carefully, said 'Very well, sir,' in the colourless voice she used on his ward rounds, and followed the two men out of the cubicle, beckoning to Nurse Wells to return as she did so.

She accompanied them, as custom dictated, to the ward doors and once through them wished the professor a brisk good morning, to be rewarded by a dark stare. 'I should be glad of a cup of coffee, Sister.'

Julia gave him a limpid look. 'Why, of course, professor,' she spoke in the tones of a much-tried hostess, 'do go into the office and I'll see about it.' She looked at Dr Reed and said warmly, 'You too, Dick?'

He grinned at her and nodded and she sailed across the landing to the kitchen. Old Meg was there, brooding over the mid-morning drinks trolley. She had been at the hospital for almost all of her life and refused to move with the times; trade unions, strikes, who did what and when, had made no impression on her; she still considered herself an old-fashioned ward maid and took no notice of anyone who tried to get her to think otherwise. She looked up now and gave Julia a reluctant smile. 'Sister there ain't no cocoa—I'd like to know where it goes at night, that I would! Want yer coffee?'

'Not me, Meg—Professor van der Wagema and Dr Reed do. If I get a tray ready will you boil some milk?'

'For 'im I will,' declared Meg, 'nice gent 'e is'.

'Dr Reed?' Julia was putting cups and saucers on to a tray.

'Oh, 'im—'e's all right, no—the professor, 'e's a bit of class, asks me about me corns . . .!'

Julia's lovely eyes widened with astonishment. Meg's corns were a constant source of annoyance to her but she had never complained to anyone but Julia about them. 'Give me the push if I tells 'em,' she explained, 'though I don't mind you knowing, Sister.'

Presumably she didn't mind the professor knowing either. Perhaps, thought Julia with a soundless giggle, there was a charming side to him she hadn't been privileged to discover. She picked up the tray and carried it to her office, where the professor was sitting at her desk, writing, and Dr Reed was perched on the radiator, looking out of the window. He got up and took the tray from her as she went in but the professor didn't raise his head.

Julia smiled at Dr Reed and whisked herself out of the room again. 'Rude man,' she muttered as she closed the door.

There was a great deal to do in the ward; beds were being made, patients were being got up and arranged in chairs and once in them remembered books, spectacles and knitting which they'd left behind on their lockers which made the whole business long winded. Besides that, there were the really ill patients; Mrs Wolff with severe thyrotoxicosis, little Dolly Waters holding leukaemia at bay from week to week and young Mrs Thorpe with transverse myelitis. She was barely in her thirties with a devoted husband and two small children, and had paralysis from the waist down. Several months in a plaster cast had done no good at all, but now she was out of it and the professor was going to examine her again. He hadn't pretended that he could cure her, but neither had he drawn a gloomy picture for her to worry about and he had promised that if there was anything to be done, he would do it. Julia, helping one of the student nurses to make her bed, reflected that tiresome though he might be, his patients trusted him.

She went back to her office presently; the nurses were going to their coffee two by two, and when they got back she and Pat would have theirs, until then, she would get on with her paper work.

The professor was still in her office, writing busily, he looked up as she went in, said coolly: 'I am almost finished, Sister.' Then went on writing. She didn't go away but stood by the door, watching him. He looked tired; after all, he was no longer a young man and even his good looks couldn't disguise the fact; she was still annoyed with him about his rejection of her offer of coffee and food, but a pang of something like pity shot through her, instantly doused by his cool: 'Pray don't stand there, Sister Mitchell, there must be something you can do and I shall be a few minutes still.'

'Oh, there is plenty.' She matched her coolness with his, although she was put out. 'Only it's all on my desk and you're still sitting at it.' She allowed a small pause before adding, 'Sir'.

He said without looking up from his writing: 'How long have we known each other, Sister?'

'Us? Oh, three years or more on this ward—you lectured me when I was a student nurse but one could hardly say that you knew me, then.'

He glanced up and smiled briefly. 'That makes me feel very old.' And then to surprise her entirely: 'How old are you, Sister Mitchell?'

She said indignantly: 'That's rather a rude question . . .'

'Why?'

'Well, wouldn't you think it rude if I were to ask you that?'

'Not in the least,' his voice was bland. 'I'm forty-one and looking forty-two in the face. I don't imagine you are forty yet?'

She gasped with annoyance. 'Of course I'm not, if you must know I'm thirty—today.'

'Many happy returns of the day.' He finished his writing and sat back to study her. 'I must say that you don't look your age.'

'Thank you for nothing, Professor.' Her green eyes flashed with temper. 'I find this a very pointless conversation and I have a great deal of work to do . . .'

He got up slowly. 'When are you and young Longman getting married?'

She blushed and hated herself for it. 'I don't know—there's plenty of time . . .'

He sauntered to the door. 'Oh, no there isn't—once you are thirty, the years fly by.' He opened the door. 'I'll be in to see Mrs Collins this afternoon. Good morning to you, Sister.'

Her 'Good morning, sir,' was snappish to say the least.

But she forgot him almost at once as she became immersed in her work; there were always forms to fill in, requests to write, the off duty to puzzle out; she worked steadily for half an hour or so; Pat was in the ward, keeping an eye on things and presently when the nurses had been to coffee, they would have theirs and sort out the day's problems before the various housemen did their rounds. And the professor, of course; an even-tempered woman, despite the fieriness of her hair, and possessed of more than the usual amount of common sense, Julia found herself feeling sorry for him again. Of course, away from the hospital, he might be a devoted husband and father, a frequenter of night clubs, a keen theatregoer, a fervent sportsman, but it was impossible to know that. His private life was a closed book to her and she wasn't interested in looking inside, only it was a pity that he found her so irritating. And yet she knew for a fact that he had told the Senior Medical Officer that she was the best sister he had ever had to deal with. It was probably her fault, she mused, for she answered him back far too often.

She sighed, reached for the 'phone and dialled the laundry. As usual she needed more linen and as usual she was going to have to wheedle it out of them.

Pat came in presently and they drank their coffee and filled in the rest of the off duty. 'My weekend,' said Pat happily, 'I shall go home.' She poured more coffee. 'Is Dr Longman off for your weekend?'

Julia shook her head. 'No, he's going to Bristol— he's applied for the registrar's position there, and this Saturday seems to be the only day they can interview him.'

'Would you like my weekend?' asked Pat instantly, 'then you could go with him.'

'That's sweet of you Pat, but he'll be better on his own, besides what would I do there? I'd be by myself most of the time. He'll go on to his home and spend Sunday there, and I'll go home on my weekend; we can sort things out after that.'

The niggling thought that Nigel could have invited her to go to his parents' home and joined her there popped into her head to be instantly ignored as petty childishness. 'Now, how can we fit Nurse Wells in for that extra half day we owe her?'

Pat was quick to take the hint and obediently pored over the off duty; Sister Mitchell was a dear even if strict on the ward, but she tended to keep herself to herself even though she had any number of friends.

The morning wore on, much too rapidly for Julia.

Mrs Collins, though still unconscious, was showing signs of improvement, but there was no news from the police. Julia went to her midday dinner with the problem still unsolved, which made her somewhat *distraite* during that meal.

'The professor being tiresome?' asked Fiona Sedgewick, who had Women's Surgical. 'I never met such a man for casting a blight on anyone unlucky enough to be near him.'

'I pity his wife,' observed Mary Chapman, who had Children's, 'that's if he can keep one long enough . . .'

'Is he married?'

'Shouldn't think so, but what a waste, all those good looks and lolly and he has just got himself a new Rolls Royce.'

Someone giggled. 'Perhaps that's why he is so irritable—I mean, they cost a good deal, don't they?'

Julia got up. 'Well, whatever it is, he'd better cheer up before he comes this afternoon.'

The professor hadn't exactly done that when he came on to the ward an hour or so later; he was, however, scrupulously polite, listening with grave attention to what Julia had to report and at the end of a lengthy examination of Mrs Collins, politely refusing her offer of tea, watching her from under heavy lids, and then thanking her just as politely so that she looked at him with surprised face. He returned the look with a bland stare of his own before, surrounded by the lesser fry of his profession, he left the ward.

'Well,' observed Julia to the pile of notes on her desk, 'what's come over him, in heaven's name?'

She was off duty after tea and half an hour later was back at her flat. Nigel was off duty too and she had planned supper for them both; they would be able to talk at their ease. She thrust a macaroni cheese into her tiny oven and frowned as she did so. Nigel would want to talk about getting married and she felt a curious reluctance to listen to him. He had the future so tidily arranged that somehow the magic was missing. Not that she had the least idea of what magic she expected. They had been more or less engaged for a year or more; he was entirely suitable for a husband too, he would be kind and patient and considerate and they would have enough to live on . . . Her mother and father liked him and with reservations she got on well enough with his parents; perhaps she wanted too much. Certainly she had been put out when he had told her that he was going to Bristol and hadn't suggested that she should go with him, they saw little enough of each other.

She mixed a salad, did her hair again and sat down to wait.

She heard his deliberate step on the stairs presently and went to open the door, suddenly anxious that the evening should be a success. He kissed her too quickly and said: 'Sorry I'm a bit late—I got caught up on Children's. God, I'll be glad to get away from St Anne's. Keep your fingers crossed for me, Julia, and pray that I'll get that job at Bristol.'

She made a soothing rejoinder, poured him a beer and sat down opposite him. 'Bad day?' she asked.

'Lord yes, you can say that again. Professor van der Wagema may be a brilliant physician but he's a cold fish. Good with the patients, mind you and funnily enough, the children like him, but talk about a loner . . .'

'Perhaps he is overworked,' offered Julia idly.

'Not him, he works for two and it makes no

difference at all. Wonder what he is like away from St
Anne's. No one's ever seen him. Crusty old devil.' He
grinned at her. 'Something smells good?'

'It's ready, I'll dish up.'

They spent a pleasant enough evening discussing
rather vaguely, their future. 'We ought to start looking
for somewhere to live, if I get this job,' said Nigel,
'Somewhere close to the hospital of course, but we can
go home for weekends when I'm free.' He frowned
thoughtfully, 'A flat, I suppose, at least to start with,
probably the hospital will have something for us.'

'It would be nicer to live away from your work,' said
Julia.

She was a country girl, born and brought up in a
small village a few miles from Salisbury and she had
never taken to London or the city, and Bristol as far as
she could make out, was going to be another London
on a smaller scale.

'We shouldn't have much rent to pay. I'll get settled
in and you can give up this job here; the place will be
furnished so we won't have that bother.'

Julia stifled a sigh; furnishing her own home didn't
seem to her to be a bother, but perhaps it would only
be for a few months, while they looked round for
something better. A house with a garden ... She
allowed her thoughts to wander; the garden at home
would be looking gorgeous, full of dahlias and
chrysanths and the virginia creeper just turning—she
would go home on her next weekend; Nigel would be
working anyway.

'What are you thinking about?' asked Nigel.

'A garden—the garden at home. It'll be nice to see it.'

'Oh, can't you change your weekend to fit in with
me?'

'No—I'd already promised Pat Down. We'll have to try to get things sorted out later on.'

He didn't seem to mind overmuch; Julia found that provoking.

She took care to climb the stairs soberly the next morning but there was no professor to sneer at her, he came not half an hour later, though. She had taken the report, given the student nurses the gist of it and was sitting at her desk, looking without much pleasure at the view of chimney pots and tired looking trees, all she could see by sitting sideways and craning her neck. She was remembering Nigel's sedate plans for their future and his even more sedate kiss when he left soon after supper.

There must be something wrong with her, she thought a little desperately, not to appreciate a good kind man such as Nigel and of course she loved him . . .

'Well, well,' observed the professor nastily from the half open door. 'Nothing better to do than sit and stare? The devil finds work for idle hands to do.'

Julia's splendid bosom swelled with indignation. 'Well, really . . . whatever will you say next?'

'Good morning might be appropriate!'

She glared up at him; his eyes looked black they were so dark and to make matters worse he was amused.

She rose from her chair with as much dignity as she could muster. 'Good morning, Professor,' she said coldly. 'You wish to see Mrs Collins? She is still unconscious, but there are signs . . .' She gave him chapter and verse and at his nod, led the way into the ward, asking Pat in a low voice to get Dr Reed and sending the nurse with Mrs Collins away—a very new student nurse, who stared at the professor as though he were Prince Charming and sidled away reluctantly.

'Is that girl competent?' rasped the professor.

Julia shot him an affronted look. 'Nurse has been training for six months, so of course she is by no means competent, but she is sensible and understands exactly what she has to do. She has the makings of a good nurse.' She drew an annoyed breath, 'Sir'.

She could have saved her breath for he didn't appear to be listening.

Dr Reed joined them then and they went through the slow precise tests and examination. The professor was studying the chart and Julia was straightening the bed clothes when she said quietly, 'Mrs Collins' eyelids are moving.'

So they began all over again. The woman was still unconscious but this time her pupils reacted to the professor's torch. He straightened his vast person and stood looking down at her. 'Now we are getting somewhere. Reed, let's have a further lot of tests.' He looked across at Julia and smiled and she blinked at its charm.

He was back again later in the morning to do his bi-weekly round, once more coldly polite. He didn't smile once and after the round, in her office, he was bitingly sarcastic about a mislaid page of notes. They weren't in the least important, for the patient was going home in the morning and they had probably got put in the file in the wrong order. It annoyed Julia but it hardly merited his caustic remarks about carelessness. She accompanied him to the ward doors and went back to her office and found the page almost at once. She put it neatly in to its place and said crossly, 'Tiresome little man . . .'

'Tiresome I may be,' said the professor from somewhere behind her, 'but you could hardly call me little.'

She swung round to face him, but before she could say anything, he added mildly, 'I believe that I left my pen here.'

Julia took a surging breath, clenched her teeth on the heated remark she was about to make and handed him the pen. He took it from her with a brief thank you, advised her coldly not to allow her feelings to get the better of her, and went away again. 'I swear I'll throw something at you next time we meet,' said Julia. Her habitual calm common sense had quite deserted her, it was a good thing that Pat went for her weekend after tea, for it meant that Julia was on duty until the night staff came on duty, and she had no time to indulge in any feelings.

Nigel was going by train to Bristol but because he was getting a lift by car from a friend who lived in Yeovil, he had chosen to take a train from Waterloo in the morning, and Julia had given herself a morning off duty so that she might see him on his way. It was an off duty she loathed for it meant coming back on duty at half-past twelve and a long, long day stretching out before her. All the same she left the ward at ten o'clock, tore into her street clothes and met Nigel outside the hospital. There wasn't much time, they took a taxi and got to the station with only a few minutes to spare.

The train was full and Nigel, a sensible man, didn't waste his time on unnecessarily protracted goodbyes; he gave her a quick kiss, with one eye prudently on the empty seats which were left, and then got into the train. There hadn't been time to say much, thought

Julia, smiling the fatuous smile people always smile at railway stations, really it had been a bit silly of her to come . . . She went close to the window where Nigel had been lucky enough to get a seat and called, 'Good luck; I'm sure everything will be fine.' She didn't go on, for Nigel was frowning a little; he disliked the showing of feelings in public, so she retreated a few paces and stood well back and since she couldn't glue her eyes to Nigel all the time, looked around her. No more than twenty yards away Professor van der Wagema was standing, a hand on the shoulder of a boy of ten or eleven, standing beside him. As she looked, he gave the boy a gentle shove, said something to him, and watched him get on to the train. The boy was in school uniform and there were other boys too. Julia looked from him to the professor and encountered a bland stare which sent the colour to her cheeks and her eyes back to Nigel. The train began to move and she made rather a thing of waving to Nigel who wasn't taking any notice.

CHAPTER TWO

SHE walked away from the professor as she waved, and
stood watching the train out of sight; hopefully he
would be gone when she turned round and started
back down the platform.

Nothing of the kind; he was coming towards her and
since she was at the end of the platform by now there
was nowhere else to go, she had to walk back.

His 'Good morning, Julia,' took her completely by
surprise; he had never called her anything other than
Sister or Sister Mitchell. She said, 'Good morning,' in
a rather faint voice and went on walking and he turned
and walked with her, for all the world, she thought
indignantly, as though he was sure of his welcome.

'Why didn't you go with Longman?' he wanted to
know.

She suppressed a strong wish to tell him to mind his
own business.

'He's got an interview in Bristol for a registrar's
post. Of course, you know that already . . .'

'Of course. I asked why you hadn't gone with him.'

She had the ridiculous urge to tell him that Nigel
hadn't asked her to. 'Well, I would have been on my
own for most of the weekend . . .' And that's a silly
thing to say she thought—she could expect some
cutting remark about interviews only taking a couple
of hours. But he didn't say anything like that. 'I've
just seen my son off to school, will you have a cup of
coffee with me?'

She stopped to look at him. 'Well, it's very kind of you—I'm on duty at one o'clock though.'

'It's just half-past ten,' he assured her, grave-faced, 'I've my car here, we can go somewhere quieter for ten minutes or so.'

'Very well,' said Julia, feeling her way; any minute he might change back into the coldly polite man she worked for, but he didn't, he commented upon the splendid weather, the horror of large railway stations, the difficulty of parking and all she had to do was to murmur suitably.

She had seen his car before, of course, but only from her office window or sliding silently past her in the forecourt. This'll be something to tell the girls, she thought as she got into the dark blue Rolls, only they'll never believe me.

The professor drove through the streaming traffic with a monumental calm which aroused her admiration. She was an indifferent driver herself, driving the rather elderly Rover through the country lanes around her home, although she much preferred her bike or even her two feet. Ever since the time she had rammed the butcher's van on a tricky corner, her nerve had suffered. Driving through London must be a nightmare; she said so now.

'Indeed,' agreed the professor politely, 'but one gets used to it—one has to.' They were driving down Gower Street and she wondered where they were going and wasn't left long in doubt—the British Museum Coffee Shop. He parked by a vacant meter and ushered her through the book shop and the shop behind that which sold reproductions and into the restaurant itself. The two shops were quite full but the restaurant wasn't. He pulled out a chair for her at a table for two and went to fetch their coffee. 'Anything to eat?' he asked over his shoulder.

She shook her head; she found him difficult to talk to, after years of being on her guard against his testy manner and cold politeness she had seldom been at a loss to answer him then, now she found herself tongue-tied. Common sense came to her aid as he sat down opposite to her; she was used to difficult situations on the ward, dealing with awkward patients and visitors, wheedling new housemen to take her advice, listening patiently to the woes of a student nurse whose love life wasn't working out. Did the professor have a love life, she wondered?

They passed each other the sugar and sipped their coffee. The professor sat at his ease, content to be silent, possibly waiting for her to take her share in the conversation. 'How old is your son?' she asked.

'Eleven. I usually drive him back to school but I have several engagements this weekend. Martha had no time this morning to take him to the station and I could cancel a meeting I was to attend far more easily than she could leave the house.'

Martha, mused Julia, a suitable name for the wife of a man such as he, she would be mouselike with wispy hair and no dress sense and always do exactly what he wanted. Pour soul ... probably there were several more children at home. Her imagination, which was vivid, conjured up a pitiful picture of a poor hard working Martha trying to please the professor. A hopeless task. She would have to talk about something else before she got too indignant.

'You have a Dutch name,' she observed and was halted by his silky reply.

'But of course—I am a Dutchman.' He sat back in

his chair, looking at her. 'And you, Julia, are very very English.'

'Well, of course I am. What makes you say that?'

'It would take too long to tell you. Dick Reed seems much happier about Mrs Collins.'

The sudden turn in conversation made her blink. All the same, she managed composedly. 'Yes, he is! There's still no news about her family though.'

'We shall have to have patience.'

She drank the rest of her coffee and began to put on her gloves 'The coffee was nice,' she told him sedately, 'thank you, Professor. You won't mind if I leave you here.'

'Yes, I do mind. I'll drive you back to St Anne's. I shall be going past the hospital in any case.'

There was no point in arguing, she got into the car again and he drove the short distance to the wide gates and leant across to open the door for her. He hadn't spoken once since they had left the coffee shop. She thanked him quickly and got out on to the pavement, adding a brief goodbye.

His dark eyes rested on her for a moment. 'It has passed an aimless hour,' he said blandly and drove away. Julia, standing and watching the big car thrust its way smoothly through the traffic, very nearly stamped a foot. 'An aimless hour, indeed,' she muttered furiously, 'I just happened to be handy, did I to while away a bit of time before he tools off to wherever he's going? And why didn't he go home and drink his coffee with the pitiful Martha?' She was so busy thinking about it that she quite forgot Nigel. It was over their midday dinner that Fiona wanted to know at what time he was to have his interview; Julia found herself blushing with guilt because she hadn't given it a thought. 'Oh—two o'clock, I think,' she said hastily, and nodded her head when Fiona observed that of course he would be ringing her later on that day. Nigel hadn't said anything of the sort. But why should he? He had had a lot on his mind and she forgave him for forgetting. Very likely he would 'phone from his parents' house. The thought cheered her up as she went on duty.

There was plenty of work, medical wards might not be as dramatic as the surgical ones, but they were just as busy, more so, for there were treatments going on all the time and three medicine rounds a day. She missed Pat although she had a part-time staff nurse until five o'clock and a second staff nurse to come on until the night staff came on duty at eight o'clock. She was tired when she got off duty, but satisfied: Mrs Collins was definitely coming out of her coma and once she was fit to understand and speak a little, they would be able to find out who she was. It was going to be a long job, but well worth it; the nasal feeding, the bed bathing, the constant turning, the gentle physio- therapy. It was a good thing, thought Julia, that there weren't many really ill patients in the ward, although as fast as one patient went home another took her place, and if she were a heart or chest case, then there would be several days of careful nursing on top of the constant routine.

The day which had been so fine had clouded over by the evening and it had begun to rain. There was a rumble of thunder too as she hurried back to her flat, with luck she would be indoors before she got soaked to the skin. She was going up the shabby steps to the front door when her eye caught a movement in the dusty patch of grass under the front window. She went down the steps again, oblivious of the rain, to see what it was. A kitten—a very small one—bedraggled and far too thin. She picked it up and it mewed soundlessly at her.

'Lost are you?' Julia tucked the animal under one arm and went up the stairs to her own small flat. It was no weather to go round knocking on doors asking if anyone had lost a kitten, indeed, she suspected that it had been dumped. She found a saucer, filled it with milk and watched the kitten drink. It was certainly half starved, its fur dirty and dull. She found an old woollen scarf and lined the lid of her work basket with it and put the little beast in it. It went to sleep at once leaving her free to get her supper.

It was while she was eating it that she decided to 'phone Nigel and presently went down to the call box in the hall. She had to wait for a minute or so before anyone answered and it was his mother's voice asking who was ringing.

'Julia—I wondered if Nigel had got to you yet . . .'

'Hours ago,' said Mrs Longman, 'he's gone down to the pub with his father.' She had a light voice which exactly suited her small slender person; when Julia was with her she felt like a carthorse. She said uncertainly: 'I wondered—that is, did he get the job?'

'Oh, my dear, yes. He did say something about 'phoning you but by the time we had had tea, it must have slipped his mind.'

'Well, that's splendid news,' Julia made her voice cheerful, 'I can't stay to talk now, have a nice weekend. Bye.'

She went back upstairs and washed her few dishes and since the kitten had woken up, gave him another saucer of warm milk and bread. 'If no one wants you,' she promised him, 'I'll have you. You'll have to be alone quite a bit, but that's better than sitting out in the rain, isn't it?'

The evening stretched emptily before her, she turned on the T.V. and watched a programme without seeing any of it, her thoughts busy.

Next weekend she would go home and take the kitten in a basket; old Gyp her father's labrador and her mother's two cats would do him no harm and he might be glad of their company. She washed her hair and had a shower and sat down again in her dressing gown, the kitten on her knee. She gave it one of her fingers to nibble and allowed her thoughts to wander and was surprised to discover after a few minutes that she wasn't thinking about Nigel at all but the professor—home with his wife, she hoped, he might even have taken her out for the evening—dinner somewhere rather grand and dancing afterwards. One didn't expect someone with a name like Martha to dance well, but probably she was quite super at it. There would be a mother's help or an au pair to look after the other children, of course, although surely with a Rolls Royce, the professor would be able to afford a Norland Nanny? She frowned; he wasn't all that young, the boy he had seen off to school that morning could have been the youngest child, the others would be teenagers . . .

She got up and put the kitten back on the scarf. It was asleep again but she addressed it none the less; it was nice to have something to talk to. 'I'm getting soft in the head,' she observed, 'sitting here doing nothing and thinking a load of nonsense. I shall go to bed.'

Which she did, to be joined presently by the kitten, who climbed laboriously on to the duvet and settled up against her.

She was up earlier than usual the next morning, so that she had time for a more leisurely breakfast before attending to the kitten's wants and going on duty. The storm had left the streets fresh and revived the dusty shrubs and trees along the street. Being a Sunday, there was no one to be seen, even the main street, usually bustling with traffic by half-past seven, was deserted. Julia made her way up to the ward to be met by the night staff nurse with the news that Professor van der Wagema was on the ward.

'In that case, I'll just see what he wants,' said Julia. Dick Reed had a weekend and perhaps there had been an admission during the night. She hung up her cape and asked the staff nurse.

'No, Sister—it's Mrs Collins—Peter Miller 'phoned the professor and he came in. Peter came to see her about six o'clock because I asked him to. She opened her eyes and grunted.'

'Good work, Staff. I'll be back in a minute.'

She went down the ward, wishing her patients good morning as she went, and slipped behind Mrs Collins' curtains. The professor, in slacks and a sports shirt and not looking in the least like a professor, was sitting on the end of the bed, writing Mrs Collins' notes. He looked human as he sat there, so that Julia said, 'Good morning, sir,' with a good deal more warmth than normal. 'Is there anything you want?' she added.

He raised his eyes from his notes and she was struck by their cold darkness. 'Thank you, no, Sister. Only to be left in peace. If I need anything or anyone, I will say so.'

There was absolutely no answer to that, although she could think of several remarks she longed to make. With a surge of annoyance she went back down the ward. Had he really called her Julia and given her coffee and driven her around in his beautiful Rolls? She must have dreamt the lot.

She took the report and sent the night nurses off duty and went back into the ward to check on the breakfasts. There would be a part time staff nurse on duty at nine o'clock and she had Nurse Wells, who was sensible anyway, as well as two student nurses. Leaving Nurse Wells in the ward she gave a quick report and sent them back to start on the morning's chores before running through the report once more with Nurse Wells. It being Sunday there was less paperwork; no laundry to argue with, no Path Lab to make appointments with. She tidied her desk and went into the ward to help with the beds and presently, the treatments. It was almost an hour before the professor came down the ward. Julia, in the middle of an argument with an elderly heart patient who could see no good reason for getting out of her bed, was interrupted by his: 'A word with you, if you please, Sister.'

She beckoned the staff nurse to take her place and walked with him to her office. Inside he waved her to her chair at the desk and sat down himself on the radiator. 'Coffee?' he enquired.

Julia, about to sit, got up again and crossed over to the kitchen where luckily Meg had the coffee ready. She bore the tray back with, her set it on the desk and sat herself down again, and since the professor had nothing to say she poured it out and handed him a cup.

'I've had no breakfast,' he observed, and as she remained silent, 'Not that it is any concern of yours, Sister.'

'None at all, sir. You wished to tell me something?'

His dark eyes gleamed beneath their lids. 'Yes. But there is another matter. Mrs Collins roused sufficiently to tell me something of herself. I have the details here, they may not be accurate; it has taken me all of two hours to get them—she still has periods of unconsciousness. I'd be glad if you will get on to the police and do everything necessary. I shall want an accurate report of her periods of consciousness. Anything out of the normal run of things I wish to know at once. You have my 'phone number.'

Julia sipped her coffee. 'Yes, I have. Four hourly T.P.R., and blood pressure?'

'Yes.' He passed his cup and she refilled it. He asked abruptly: 'You have heard from Longman?'

She hadn't expected that and she was betrayed into saying no, before she said yes. At his raised eyebrows she added lamely, 'I 'phoned last night. He's got the post.'

'Yes. He seemed pleased . . .'

'He 'phoned you?' she asked in surprise.

'No—I happened to be with Doctor Lamborne when he rang him.'

He finished his coffee and stood up. 'I suppose we shall be losing you very shortly.'

Her green eyes glinted. 'You will find Staff Nurse Down will make an excellent sister.'

'I shall look forward to that,' he told her blandly as he went.

She had no time for anything but the ward for the rest of the day; the police came and so, after lunch, did the visitors and treatments and medicines had to be fitted in despite these interruptions. She went off duty late but satisfied; the police had unearthed a niece of

Mrs Collins who would come the next day. She had sounded pleasant enough on the 'phone and seemed concerned enough about her aunt. And Mrs Collins had gone steadily ahead. Julia shaking the dust of twenty-four patients from her feet went thankfully back to her flat, where the kitten, looking more like a kitten now, greeted her with pleasure, ate supper and curled up again on its scarf, while Julia showered and got into a cotton dress and cooked her own supper. Tomorrow evening she and Nigel would go out for a meal but just now she was content to spend a quiet evening and if she had half hoped that he would ring her she ignored the thought. He would be back sometime that evening, but he had warned her that it might be in the early hours of the morning. She read the Sunday papers, and paused every now and then to mull over the memory which nagged like a sore tooth; the professor was looking forward to someone else in her place, he couldn't wait for her to go. She felt unreasonably hurt about that. Thank heaven that Nigel had got the job; they could have a quiet wedding soon, he would need only a couple of months to settle in and even if they had to find a flat outside the hospital, it shouldn't take all that long; anything would do for a start, they would only be renting it and they could move if it didn't suit them. She sat weaving plans for the future and presently, accompanied by the kitten, went to bed.

It was the professor's round in the morning. She greeted him in a cool, wooden voice, agreed that Mrs Collins' troubles seemed to be almost over, discussed Mrs Winter's unfortunate habit of ignoring her diet, filled in a number of X-Ray forms and Path Lab requests and finally ushered her party out of the ward,

where the lesser fry went about their business and
the professor and Dick Reed went into her office
where they continued their discussions and drank
several cups of coffee while Julia sat between them,
passing the biscuit tin to and fro and making notes
obediently when told to do so. When finally they got
to their feet the professor said: 'Go on ahead will
you, Dick?' He glanced at his watch, 'Sister
Sedgewick will be expecting us—I'll be with you in
a couple of minutes.'

Julia was standing behind her desk, wondering what
was coming next. She searched swiftly in her mind to
discover what could have gone wrong for it must
surely be that. The professor had been remotely civil
and no more throughout the round and probably he
was harbouring some petty grievance . . .

'Yesterday,' he told her smoothly, 'I told you that
I looked forward to seeing someone in your place; to
dismiss any misunderstandings on that point, I should
point out that it would not be for the reason which I
feel sure springs instantly to your mind.' He looked
down his magnificent nose at her. 'Women are
illogical.' He opened the door but turned to look at
her, gaping at him, as he left. 'Seen young Longman?'
he wanted to know.

She hadn't, he hadn't 'phoned either and she had
had no time to find out if he was back in the hospital.
She said coldly. 'No, I haven't. Neither of us have
much leisure . . .'

'Sarcasm does not become you, Julia.'

When he had gone, she sat down at her desk again
and stared down at the list of things, neatly tabled by
Pat, that needed attention. Presently she picked up the
'phone and began her daily battle with the laundry,

but her heart wasn't in it, there was too much on her mind.

She saw Nigel briefly on the way back from her dinner. He was so obviously delighted with himself that she hadn't the heart to ask him why he hadn't 'phoned her. 'Exactly what I want,' he told her enthusiastically, his pleasant open face beaming. He plunged into details and when he at length paused she asked: 'And is there a flat going with the job?'

'Flat? Oh yes, there's a house nearby with three flats—quite nice, I believe.'

'Didn't you go and have a look at it?'

'No, love—the whole interview and so on took much longer than I had expected and I wanted to get home.'

'Yes, of course. I rang your mother.'

'She told me. I meant to give you a ring, but my father was keen to go down to the pub and talk about things . . .'

All quite reasonable thought Julia, so why was she feeling cross? 'You're off this evening?'

He nodded. 'We'll go out, shall we, and celebrate?'

She smiled widely at him. 'Lovely. Seven o'clock by the porter's lodge?'

She had talked too long, she hurried back to the ward, happy again.

She got off duty punctually because Pat, bless her, was never late on duty. She fed the kitten, showered and poked around in her wardrobe for something to wear. There was a green thing she hadn't worn for quite a while, a straight sheath which showed off her figure to perfection, and highlighted her hair. She didn't look too bad, she conceded and remembered to put on a pair of only moderately high heels. Nigel and she were exactly the same height but if she wore the high heels she preferred she topped him by an inch or so and he didn't like it. She had plenty of time, she sat down for a little while, the kitten on her lap. 'I must get you a basket tomorrow,' she told him, 'and give you a name.' She thought for a minute, 'I found you in this street, didn't I? So you'll be Wellington.'

She kissed his small furry head, picked up her purse and with her loose coat over her shoulders, went back to the hospital. Nigel was there and, most annoyingly, so was Professor van der Wagema, talking to him.

They paused in their talk to wish her a good evening, remark upon the delightful night, and then resume their conversation. Julia, standing between them, with Nigel's hand on her shoulder, listened with half an ear. Nigel admired the professor and although they rarely had much to do with each other they seemed to have found a great deal to talk about. She was enlightened about this presently: 'Professor van der Wagema knows my new chief very well,' Nigel told her. 'They were up at Cambridge together.'

'How interesting.' Julia, wanting her dinner, just managed not to look at the big clock on the wall in front of her, while the professor, listening with grave attention to what Nigel was saying, studied her charming person from under heavy lids.

When the conversation had broken up and Nigel and Julia went on their way, Nigel enthused about the professor while they drove through the busy streets to the small restaurant in Old Bailey which they invariably patronised. It was fairly near to the hospital for one thing and the food was French and fairly cheap and since they had been eating there for a year or more, they were given a corner table where they could talk in peace. Nigel was still extolling the professor's brilliance as they sat down. 'Pity you two don't get on,' he observed cheerfully, 'although he has a great opinion of you as a nurse. Told me the ward wouldn't be the same without you.'

'Well,' said Julia reasonably, 'he'll just have to get used to that, won't he? Pat will step into my shoes when I leave.'

She broke off to study the menu; since this was by way of being a celebration she chose rather lavishly and sipped the iced Dubonnet she had asked for. 'You always have sherry,' commented Nigel.

'I want something different this evening. After all, we're celebrating, aren't we?'

He beamed at her. 'Rather. I start at the beginning of November, that gives them time to get another man to replace me. We could get married next summer.'

'Next summer?' The surprise in her voice made him look up. 'But that's months away. Why can't we have a quiet wedding this autumn—it's almost October already Nigel. Why do we have to wait?'

He smiled and took her hand on the table. 'Look, darling, it's good sense to wait a bit; I can save up a little and so can you and I can work my way in before you come—I'll know a few people by then and you won't be lonely.'

'But I won't be lonely with you,' she protested.

'I'll be working hard all day, most days,' he pointed out patiently. 'Mother thought it a very good idea. I can go home for my weekends when I get them so I shan't get bored.'

'And me?' asked Julia, forgetting her grammar in the urgency to make him see sense. 'What about me?'

'Well you can come down to Mother's—you'll be due some leave again soon, won't you?'

It wasn't at all what she'd planned; it seemed to her that their future was being taken out of their hands and arranged by his mother, but it was no good rushing her fences, she would have to think of something . . .

'I dare say that would be a good idea,' she said quietly and was rewarded by his contented smile.

They didn't talk any more about their future that evening; Nigel still had a lot to tell her about his new job, it took up the whole of dinner, and he was still explaining the layout of the hospital in Bristol when he stopped the car outside her little flat.

'Coming up for coffee?' asked Julia, and added, 'I've got a kitten, he's called Wellington.'

'You'll have to find him a home when you come down to Bristol,' said Nigel. 'They don't allow cats or dogs.'

The resentment which had been smouldering just below the surface all the evening gave her eyes an emerald glint. 'Oh, indeed? In that case we'll have to find somewhere else to live. I'll not give him away.'

Nigel laughed tolerantly. 'You'll change your mind, darling—you can hardly turn your back on a flat with all mod cons for the sake of a cat.'

'No?' She put her head through the window and he kissed her. 'Thanks for a lovely evening, Nigel. See you around. I'm going home this weekend.'

He hadn't said he would come in for coffee and just at that moment she didn't particularly want him to. She was being silly about Wellington, but he could at least have sympathised and tried to think of a way out. The kitten came to meet her as she opened her door and she picked him up and wandered restlessly round her room while he arranged himself round her neck, purring into her ear. 'Don't worry,' she told him, 'I'll not part with you.'

In bed later, common sense came to her rescue; she had been edgy all the evening, they had got off to a bad start, from her point of view at least, with the professor making an unwelcome third at their meeting, and Nigel's mother and her tiresome plans . . . No, it went back further than that; she had been put out because Nigel had gone off to Bristol on his own when she could so easily have gone with him if only he'd asked her in time. It'll be all right tomorrow, she promised herself and slept on the thought.

She didn't see Nigel at all during the next day; he would be operating for most of the day and she was kept busy with a couple of admissions and lengthy sessions with Mrs Collins' niece, who, although kind hearted and sensible, quite obviously didn't want the bother of arranging her aunt's future.

'It won't be for some time yet,' Julia pointed out reasonably, 'Mrs Collins isn't fit to move and won't be for several weeks. We don't expect you to make a home for her, the social worker attached to the hospital is willing to find out about some sort of accommodation for her, not too far from you, if possible. What we really want to get straight is if you could deal with her possessions and pay up her landlady and so on? Social Security will help you financially . . .'

It was a relief to have things settled at last; she told Dick Reed when he came on the ward later and went with him to see the two new patients. Chest cases both of them. He spent some time examining them, wrote up their notes, expressed the opinion that they would do well enough until the professor's round on Thursday, and then went away again.

Julia, who loved her work, decided that evening that she needed a holiday, she was getting stale and vaguely discontented; not like her at all. There had been tentative plans for her to go to Portugal with Fiona and Mary, sometime in October, but she didn't think that was what she wanted. Home would be the best place—a week or ten days pottering round with her mother, riding in the mornings, going to the rather staid dinner parties their elderly friends gave from time to time and spending days with friends of her own age who she so seldom saw nowadays. She thought about it all the next day, discussed it with Fiona and Mary and quite made up her mind. It only remained for her to tell Nigel and she could do that when they next spent an evening together; if he could manage it, he could spend a weekend . . .

Her plans buoyed her up all the next day and even the wet early morning dreariness of Thursday morning couldn't depress her. She prepared for the professor's round with more than usual briskness and greeted him cheerfully. His response, as usual, was coolly polite but she hardly noticed that. The round went well even if it was rather protracted and presently he and Dick Reed drank their coffee while they discussed their patient's conditions, adding instructions to those Julia already had, handing her endless signed forms for her to fill in. They had just finished when Dick Reed was called away to an admission in Casualty. The professor made no move from the radiator where he was sitting. 'Let me know if you want me, Dick,' he advised and when the door had closed behind his Registrar: 'You look tired, Julia, you need a holiday.'

She looked up from the notes she was tidying on the desk. 'Well, I'm going to have one,' she told him with satisfaction. 'I'm going home for ten days in a couple of weeks' time.'

'And where is home?' The question was so idly put that she answered without thought. 'Near Salisbury—along the Chalke Valley—it's a small village. Stratford Bissett . . .'

'A delightful name. Your father lives there?'

'Yes, he's a retired schoolmaster, at least not quite retired, he takes boys in their holidays for cramming and visits two prep schools each week.' She suddenly realised that she was giving away a whole lot of information to someone who couldn't be in the least interested, and came to an abrupt halt.

Her companion didn't seem to notice, he went on, almost lazily. 'You have brothers and sisters?'

She reflected that they had known each other for more than three—almost four—years and never once had he evinced any interest in her as a person. She said 'Yes,' and that was all.

He couldn't have been all that interested; he got up after a few moments, reminded her that he would be taking a teaching round the next afternoon and went away.

He was at his most remote when he arrived on the ward the following day accompanied by half a dozen students. And two can play at that game, she decided, though the students, all anxious to be at their best and nervous, must regard her as a martinet of the most horrifying kind. All the same, she managed to help them out when the professor wasn't looking, with nods and winks to put them on the right track. At the end of the round the professor was kind enough to observe that they had done quite well, even allowing for Sister Mitchell's well meant hints.

She had reddened delightfully at that, but had said nothing.

She had bought a basket for Wellington and in order to save time had packed an overnight bag on Friday morning before she went on duty, with any luck she would be able to get an evening train to Salisbury. If she 'phoned home just before she left her father would meet her there. She went through the day happily enough, now that she knew she would be free in a few hours. She had seen Nigel at dinner time, just for a few minutes and suggested that he might get a weekend while she was on holiday and drive himself down to her home and he had seemed delighted with the idea. They had made a date for Monday evening when they would both be off duty, and she had returned to the afternoon's work in a glow of contentment.

It had taken no time at all to hurry round to the flat once she was off duty, change into a jersey two-piece, cram Wellington into his basket and with her overnight bag in her other hand, take a taxi to Waterloo. It was still early evening and quite warm and the train was only half full. She sat with Wellington's basket beside her, and allowed her thoughts to dwell on the future. It seemed rosy enough although there were one or two small pinpricks, silly ones really—her future mother-in-law loomed a little too large but she was the first to admit that probably she was making a mountain out of a molehill. She still could not see why she and Nigel shouldn't get married before Christmas, perhaps if he spent a couple of days with her while she was on holiday she would be able to persuade him. Then there was the vexed question of her birthday. It had undoubtedly slipped Nigel's mind, he had had a lot to think about just then, all the same, she had been hurt, still was . . . One day soon, she told herself bracingly, she would tell him about it and they would laugh together.

The train drew into Salisbury and she collected her bag and with Wellington's basket in her hand, got out of the carriage. She saw her father at once, tall and thin and a little stooping and her heart gave a happy leap; for some reason she was glad to be well away from St Anne's and her own problems, which already seemed remote and unimportant. She gave a small yelp of delight and hurried towards him.

CHAPTER THREE

MR MITCHELL embraced his daughter warmly, took her bag and led her outside to where the car, an elderly Rover stood. 'Your mother's at home,' he told her, 'dishing up the fatted calf. It seems a long time since you were home, my dear.'

'Four weeks, Father—Nigel had a weekend when I did and we went to his home, if you remember. I'm going to have ten days' holiday in a couple of weeks, and he'll come home for his weekend if you and Mother don't mind.'

They had got into the car and her father was fiddling with his seat belt. 'You know we love to have you. Madge 'phoned to say she'd come over for the day and bring Harry with her.'

'Oh, good, I haven't seen him for ages. Has he any teeth yet?'

They exchanged small items of news as they drove out of the city and took the road to Stratford Bissett and the road along the Chalke Valley. It was almost dark by now and the car's headlights shone on the hedges on either side of the road, presently they revealed a handful of cottages as they passed through a small village. Half a mile along the road Mr Mitchell turned the car in through an open gateway and stopped before his front door. The house was in darkness now, but Julia knew every inch of it; stone and flint with a low tiled roof and lattice windows and tall twisted chimneys and a solid door with a wide

46

porch with seats on either side worn smooth by generations of use. She got out of the car and ran inside, down the flagstoned hall to the kitchen. Her mother was at the table, putting the finishing touches to supper and she looked up and smiled as Julia went in.

'Darling, how lovely to see you. Is that the kitten your father was telling me about? He'll be hungry, poor little scrap. We'll shut the doors and he can have his supper with Gyp and Muffin and Maud. Take your jacket off, dear, supper's just ready.'

Julia gave her mother a hug, tossed her jacket into a chair, shut the door and let Wellington out of his basket. Gyp, her father's dog, had lumbered over to greet Julia, now she put her great head down and blew gently over the kitten who backed away and then crept up close to the dog.

Julia watched them. 'Oh, good, Gyp will look after him. Isn't it splendid that Nigel's got his job at Bristol? Of course, I knew he would, all the same, it's pretty super.'

Her mother agreed. 'You'll be able to get married now . . .'

'Well, he wants to wait until next summer—so that he can get settled in.'

Julia was picking bits off the quiche lorraine her mother had just put on the table and she didn't look up.

'Surely . . .' began her mother and changed it to: 'That'll give you nice time to find somewhere to live.'

'Oh, there is a flat that goes with the job—furnished too.'

Julia could almost hear her mother thinking and changed the conversation smartly. 'I've got ten days'

holiday, Mother. Will it be all right if I come home?
In about two weeks' time?' She turned to smile at her
father as he came into the room. 'Nigel could get a
weekend off, I expect.'

'That'll be lovely, darling. Do you want to go up to
your room, or shall I dish up?'

'Give me five minutes. Don't let Wellington escape,
will you?'

She slept soundly that night, but she always did in the
country. Wellington curled up beside her; none the
worse for meeting Muffin and Maud, who were both
elderly anyway and tolerant of kittens. Besides, Gyp
had taken him under her wing and he had eaten a
splendid supper with the three of them.

The fine weather held, Julia got up early dressed in
old slacks and a disreputable sweater and crossed the
garden, and the small paddock beyond, to the stables
where the old pony Star, and Jane the donkey lived. It
was only just light but they were pleased to see her,
she saddled Star and then rode him out of the gate and
into the lane beyond to take the bridle path across the
fields towards the village. There was no one about
although she could hear a tractor in the distance and
the church in the village striking the hour. She was
utterly at peace, in a bubble of contentment, her
thoughts so quiet as to be almost nonexistent. She
gave Star a rest at the top of the slope behind the
house and sat looking at the broad sweep of country
before her, wide green fields, ploughed ones too and
winding in and out between them the little river
Nadder. She found herself shocked and surprised to
discover that she was wishing that she could show it
all to Professor van der Wagema. She had no idea why

she should have thought of him and she forgot him almost as soon as they had turned for home. Star, with the prospect of a rub down and breakfast, trotted along sturdily, anxious to be back in the paddock with his companion and Julia let Jane out before she began on him. It was bright sunlight and pleasantly warm by the time she had finished with him and as she went back to the house she could smell bacon cooking. She wrinkled her lovely nose and sighed: there was a lot to be said for living in the country, on the other hand she loved her job . . .

The two days passed all too quickly, it seemed to her that in no time at all she was climbing the stairs to her flat with Wellington muttering in his basket; he was going to hate being cooped up in one room as much as she was. Perhaps Nigel was right in saying that he shouldn't go to Bristol with them; he could always go to her home, he had settled down quickly enough there. On the other hand she wanted to keep him.

The room was stuffy and she opened a window and made tea before getting supper for the two of them and presently she went to bed.

There hadn't been any admissions while she had been away and the two chest cases were a little better. Three patients would be going home before lunch and Dick Reed had already 'phoned to say that he wanted the beds by the afternoon. Julia made sure that they were ready and after her usual round went to take a look at Mrs Collins. Decidedly better, wide awake and even trying to talk. Julia went off to her office, well pleased and rang Dick Reed to find out what exactly was coming into the empty beds.

'A query coronary for observation, a nephritis and a leukaemia. I'll be up to see them—let me know as soon as you've got them will you?'

They were all ill, indeed the leukaemia looked as though she wouldn't last another day, but Julia had seen such cases before; a blood transfusion and rest and good food, and the patient would be able to carry on again at least for a time. She accompanied Dick Reed when he came to examine them and then left him in the office to write up his notes while she gave out the medicines. It was almost six o'clock by the time she got off duty and she was tired. But she shook the tiredness off as she walked back to the flat. Nigel would be coming round presently and she wanted to have a meal ready for him. It would have to be ham and salad, there wasn't time to prepare more; she stopped at the delicatessen on the corner, bought what she needed and hurried to see Wellington, shower and change into a blouse and skirt and lay the table. The room looked pleasant with a small table lamp alight, highlighting the flowers she had brought back with her; the right setting for a talk about the future.

Nigel came a little after eight o'clock and she saw at once that he was tired. 'You've had a busy day.' Her quiet voice was sympathetic, 'Sit down and have a glass of beer before supper.'

He went over his day's work then; a tricky operation he wasn't very happy about, a bad road crash which had upset the theatre list, one of the theatre nurses fainting . . .

'A real Monday,' commented Julia, 'what a blessing it's Tuesday tomorrow.'

He laughed and caught her hand and kissed her.

'You're too good to be true sometimes, Julia. I don't think I know the real you underneath that serenity.'

It struck her forcibly that he didn't; she had tried hard to batten down the occasional fiery moments of temper. It was a shock to realise that the only person who knew of her occasional flashes of rage was the professor, and that was because he was invariably the cause of them.

She didn't mention their future while they had supper, only when she had cleared the table and put the coffee tray between them did she ask: 'Heard any more about the new job?'

She shouldn't have said it. He said irritably: 'How could I possibly? You know as well as I do that it takes a couple of weeks at least for the official letter to be sent.'

He drank his coffee and sat back and presently his eyes closed and he slept. Julia, although disappointed, wasn't in the least put out; he'd had a long day and things hadn't gone right and probably he'd have to be up during the night as well. She sat quietly, allowing her thoughts to wander. Her own day had gone well enough and she'd had a weekend at home too. She smiled, remembering Madge and small Harry. Madge was five years younger than she, small and dark and pretty, they were so unalike that those who didn't know them never believed that they were sisters. It will be nice to be married, mused Julia and have children and a home, although it might be some time before she had a home of her own choosing. Madge had gone straight to Jim's farmhouse and spent a happy six months changing the curtains and carpets and polishing the furniture, handed down from one generation to the next and then, content with her surroundings, she had produced Harry. The first, she assured Julia, of the family she intended to have. 'At least two boys,' she had said seriously, 'Jim's buying more land and there'll be something for them—and a girl or two to even things up.' Julia felt a pang of envy; she doubted whether Nigel would want more than one child—two, perhaps, and she would have to have them quickly. She frowned fiercely, thirty was a depressing age . . .

Nigel had opened his eyes. 'What's the matter?'

She smiled. 'Nothing, just that I remembered that I was thirty.'

'A sensible age—they asked about you at Bristol—I forgot to tell you—they thought they might have a part-time job to offer you if you were interested. Two sisters will be retiring next summer; you could go full time if you wanted to.'

Julia sat up straight. 'But Nigel, I don't want to. You'll be getting enough for us to live comfortably without me having to work, even part time. I want to be a housewife and have a couple of babies and cook . . .'

He said easily. 'Hey, you don't need to be so indignant about it, and there's loads of time for a baby.' He shrugged, 'Of course if you're dead set on doing nothing that's fine. If you worked for a year, even, we could save all your salary and start buying a house . . .' He leaned forward and dropped a kiss on her downcast face. 'Anyway you've a matter of eight or nine months to decide, darling. And no one would guess what an old lady you are; you're really the most beautiful girl I've ever seen.'

She saw that he didn't want to discuss their future seriously. She uncurled herself from her chair and said a little too brightly: 'I'll get another cup of coffee, shall I? It'll wake you up before you go.'

He laughed. 'Being thrown out, am I?'

'That's right,' she laughed with him, uneasily aware that even if she had let him, he didn't want to stay. Not that she would have allowed him to but it would be fun to be tempted . . .

It was the professor's round the next morning. Not in the best of tempers Julia decided as he stalked into the ward, his face a bland mask, his, 'Good morning, Sister,' so crisp it was positively terse. She instantly became very professional, reciting the information he required in a precise voice and handing forms, Path Lab reports and X–ray forms just half a second before he asked for them; she felt a wicked delight in doing it, for she knew it annoyed him. He brings out the very worst in me, she thought, watching him examining the woman with leukaemia, and yet the patients doted on him. He straightened his vast bulk and before he could put out a hand she had the Path Form ready. Just for the moment his eye met hers and she could have sworn that somewhere under those composed features he was laughing.

Inevitably the conversation turned to Nigel's new job as Julia, the Professor and Dick Reed had their coffee after the round was over. 'A flat with the job,' observed the professor airily, 'do you intend to get a job there, Julia?'

After his distant manner of the ward, the airiness seemed to Julia a bit much.

'I've hardly had time to think about it,' she told him, 'time enough to decide . . .'

He gave her a long steady look. 'That's where you're wrong, but you will have to find that out for yourself.'

She stared at him, for it seemed a strange thing to say and as far as she could see there was no point in answering him.

Nigel was on call until midnight and although some of her friends had asked her to go to a film with them, she had refused. A quiet evening, she had decided, in which she could have a good think. It was fast being borne in upon her that she and Nigel were drifting towards an uncertain future neither of them was quite happy about—at least, speaking for herself, she wasn't happy.

She handed over to Pat soon after five o'clock, fetched her cloak and left the ward. It had been growing dark for the last half-hour or so—too dark for the time of year—a storm brewing; she hurried down the stairs and across the entrance hall just as the first heavy drops of rain fell. She paused at the doors, uncertain whether to make a dash for it and get wet or hang around until the storm was over. The whole sky was black now and it could last an hour or more. She decided to chance it and took a step outside to be plucked back by her cloak.

'You'll be drowned like a rat,' said the professor matter-of-factly. 'Wait here, I'll get the car and then drive you back.'

He gave her no chance to answer but had gone, walking fast to the consultants' car park close by, and when he drew up in front of the door a few moments later, she got in thankfully enough for the rain was streaming down and there had been a low grumbling of thunder.

'Where to?' asked the professor.

She told him and he nodded. 'Close by. Better than living in I dare say.'

She agreed pleasantly. 'Although the neighbourhood isn't very inviting, but it's reasonably quiet.'

There really wasn't much time for more conversation. He stopped before the house and she had to admit that in the rain and under the grey, dreary sky, it looked uninviting. She thanked him and started to open the door.

His 'Stay where you are,' was uttered in a voice which was intended to be obeyed, so she didn't move. If he chose to get wet that was his business.

He opened the door, said 'Run for it,' and shut the door behind her. On the doorstep she realised that he was beside her, opening the door and urging her inside just as a brilliant flash of lightening heralded a clap of thunder to shatter the eardrums. Julia, who was quite cowardly when it came to storms, caught the professor by the coat sleeves and buried her bright head in his chest. She remembered who he was at the last minute and shot away from him as though he had been red hot. 'Sorry,' she mumbled, 'I don't like lightning.'

He didn't answer, merely held her lightly for a moment and then said, 'Shall we go to your flat and you can take off that wet cloak?'. He pushed her gently towards the stairs. 'At the top?' he wanted to know.

She led the way and unlocked her door, to be met by a terrified Wellington, who frenziedly tried to climb up her legs. The professor shut the door behind him, removed the kitten gently, tucked him under one arm and went to close the curtains and turn on the lamp.

'That's better.' He stood in the middle of the room, making it seem very small, looking around him. 'This is where you live?' he said softly. 'I have often wondered.'

Julia had taken off her wet cloak and was pulling off her ruined cap. 'They call it a flat,' she told him, 'but of course it's really only one room with hot and cold and a cooking stove. But I'm happy here.'

'Are you? Are you really, Julia? You are an outdoor girl. You should at least have a garden . . .'

'Well, it's not for ever. Would you like a cup of coffee?'

'Yes, please.' He sat down in the chair Nigel always used and looked completely at home in it and Wellington curled up against his waistcoat, the kitten's small head buried against him. He stroked the kitten gently. 'He doesn't like storms either. Isn't he lonely all day?'

Julia was filling the kettle. 'I'm sure he is but I found him in the street a week or two ago, half starved. I took him home for my weekend and he loved it.'

The professor somehow seemed a different man, sitting there so very at ease, so much so that she was tempted to ask him if his wife wasn't expecting him home, but perhaps Martha had learnt not to ask him questions like that. She searched around in her head for a safe topic of conversation and came up with, 'Is your son happy at school?'

'Yes. He's just starting his second year. You know of the place, I expect?' He mentioned a prep school.

'Oh, of course, Father is the Latin coach there,' she said at once.

'Ah yes, you did tell me—a retired schoolmaster. Latin, Greek and Maths I presume?'

'That's right.' She turned to look at him as she spooned Nescafé into two mugs, and almost dropped the jar as the room was lighted by a blaze of blue light and a crack of thunder made everything rattle. The professor got up, still with Wellington under one arm, and took the jar from her shaking hand. 'Alarming,' he observed soothingly, 'but no damage done.' He put the jar on a shelf and reaching for the boiling kettle said, 'Sit down and take this creature, will you, while I see to this.'

She sat feeling a fool and saying so. 'Rubbish,' he told her firmly, 'besides, it's a sop to my ego that I've at last discovered a chink in your armour of chilly calm.'

She blinked at him. 'Chilly calm,' she echoed. 'I'm not . . .'

'The very epitome. The ideal ward sister in person, you wear the image like a second skin. I wonder what's underneath?'

She said distantly: 'I think you're being rather rude.'

He handed her a mug of coffee and sat down again. 'You've always thought that, haven't you?' His voice was silky.

She made haste to say: 'The storm's going away . . .'

He laughed softly: 'How providential, Julia.' He drank his coffee and got up. 'I must go, Martha will wonder what has happened to me. No, don't get up, I'll see myself out.'

He had gone before she could think of anything to say.

The storm had rumbled away and presently she got up and fed Wellington and made herself some supper. She had been going to sit quietly and ponder the future, she reminded herself, but somehow she found it difficult to concentrate on it, instead she found herself thinking about the professor. Natural curiosity, she told herself, quite forgetting that until just lately she hadn't been in the least curious about him, but then it was only just lately that he had ever bothered to talk to her. There had always been talk of a professional nature, of course, and polite nothings at Christmas and the annual hospital ball, when he had danced with her, very correctly, just once. It was a kind of unwritten law that the consultants should dance with their ward sisters and he had observed it although he had never been sufficiently carried away to repeat that performance. And as for the conversation while they drank their coffee after his rounds, that was almost always shop with the odd off-hand remark about the weather or whether she had enjoyed her holidays offered her with rather impatient politeness. He might be quite a different person, she considered, if one could get to know him and he wasn't so rude. The faint suspicion that he was rude on purpose to annoy her crossed her mind and was instantly dispelled for there was no sense in it. She dismissed his image with difficulty and got pencil and paper and started to calculate just how much money she and Nigel would need to live on, she did it neatly, so that she could show it to him next time they were together, and prove that there was really no need for her to work.

She wasn't on until one o'clock the next day, for Pat had a half-day before her days off. Nigel had an hour to spare too which meant that they could meet at the café down the street and have coffee together.

He was waiting when she got there, sitting at one of the plastic tables piled with the last customer's coffee cups and plates of crumbs. The café owner came over as she sat down, swept the debris on to a tray, gave the table a token wipe, said, 'Two coffees?' without being told anything, and then went away to get them.

Julia wrinkled her lovely nose at the smell of hot vinegar and chips. 'This place is a dump,' she observed, 'but at least it's somewhere to go.' She smiled as she spoke. 'Did you manage a quiet night?'

'Yes, not too bad. Can you get an evening tomorrow? I shall be free and there is that film we both want to see. There won't be time to eat first but we can get a sandwich and coffee afterwards.'

'Pat's got days off but it just so happens that the part-time staff nurse asked if she could work from two until eight o'clock. Couldn't be better, could it?'

Their coffee came, surprisingly good in its thick white pottery cups and they drank it slowly, talking idly. Nigel didn't mention his new job and there really wasn't time to have a serious talk about anything. They walked back to St Anne's and parted at its entrance. Nigel's, 'See you, old girl,' struck Julia as unromantic.

They met again the following evening, rather later than they had intended, so that there was only time to say hullo before hurrying to Nigel's car and driving up to the West End. There were queues outside the cinema and they joined the shortest one even though it was for the more expensive seats. 'I should have booked, but I forgot,' said Nigel, 'but I don't suppose we'll have to wait long.'

They didn't talk much, for one thing there wasn't much to talk about except their work which was hardly conversation for a public place, they exchanged a few remarks about nothing in particular and it struck Julia that other than their work they hadn't a great

deal in common, something which she had never
realised before. She looked at Nigel for a reassurance
she badly needed although she wasn't sure why, and
she got a casual smile. 'It won't be long now,' he
observed, 'I only hope it'll be worth the waiting.'

As it happened it was. Julia, coming out of the
cinema a couple of hours later was still bemused with
its splendour, and she hesitated on the pavement,
momentarily separated from Nigel by the crowds.

'Lost?' Professor van der Wagema's bland voice
sounded quietly in her ear.

'Certainly not. Nigel's here, only I can't see him for
the moment.'

'In that case, stay here and I'll find him for you.' He
turned his head and said something to a girl behind
him, then: 'You can keep each other company until I
get back.'

He disappeared into the crowd and Julia and the girl
eyed each other warily. If this was Martha, and who
else could it be, anyway, thought Julia, she had been
sadly mistaken in her guessing. This girl was only a
little younger than herself, exquisitely made up and
beautifully dressed and very, very pretty although
just at that moment she was frowning with annoyance.
I suppose I'd frown too if my husband went off
looking for someone I'd never met and left me with a
woman he hadn't even bothered to introduce, mused
Julia and tried a smile on her companion. 'Wasn't it a
splendid film?' she essayed.

'Not too bad if you like that kind of thing.' The blue
eyes rested on hers for a moment and then searched the
crowd, dismissing her. Julia, whose manners were
practised, tried again: 'I'm sorry if you are being held
up, I'm sure Professor van der Wagema won't be long...'

He came towards them as she spoke, head and shoulders above the people still milling around, and he had Nigel with him. She thanked the professor nicely and his cool, 'Not at all, Sister Mitchell,' chilled her before he took the girl's arm and cleaved a way through the crowds.

'Sorry about that, old girl,' said Nigel, 'decent of van der Wagema to come looking for me.' He took her arm. 'There's quite a good pub down the street, let's get a sandwich.'

Julia ate her sandwich and drank lager with it although she longed for a cup of tea and all the while she was wondering what the professor was doing, probably eating a delicious supper at the Savoy or somewhere equally splendid and if not that, she decided, her imagination running riot, driving home where he and his Martha would sit by the fire in a splendid drawing room, the low table between them loaded with dainty sandwiches and vol-au-vents and a silver pot of coffee—she could almost smell its fragrance.

'Hi!' Nigel sounded amused. 'You're a long way off. Have another of these cheese sandwiches. Must keep up your strength you know. We've a list as long as my arm in the morning, can't think where they all come from.'

She gave herself a mental shake and listened while he told her about the various cases and when he'd finished she asked suddenly: 'Nigel, do you ever wish you were doing something else?'

His rather serious face broke into a smile. 'Lord, no. What else could I do? And you? You wouldn't want to be anything but a nurse, would you?'

'Well, yes—I want to be a wife and have a family. Nigel I'm thirty years old . . .'

'So what? You don't look it for a start and time enough to settle down.' He grinned at her, 'I can't wait to get my teeth into this new job.'

And I, thought Julia sadly, can't wait to get married, only it looks as though I shall have to.

It was a good thing she was going on holiday soon, she decided the following morning, for she had no wish to go to work. The weather had broken and late summer had suddenly become chilly autumn. The grey damp sky had affected the patients too, true several of them were too ill to care what the weather was doing, but even Mrs Winter had lost her interest in her companions and lay back on her pillows, staring at nothing.

'And what's the matter with you?' asked Julia on her morning round.

'Me, fed up, I am, Sister. Nothing but ham and injections. Now if you was to offer me a bar of Cadbury's fruit and nut . . .'

Julia laughed gently. 'Mrs Winter I wouldn't dare do such a thing—think of the work we'd have getting you stabilised again. Besides what would Professor van der Wagema say?'

Mrs Winter brightened a bit. 'Would 'e mind? If I was to go all unconscious?'

'You bet he would, he'd probably throw me out without a reference too.'

Mrs Winter grinned. 'Now that's something 'e won't do, Sister. Not if I knows it.'

'So no chocolate, Mrs Winter,' warned Julia and went back to her office.

She had no sooner sat down than Pat put her head through the door. 'Time for a cup of coffee?' she asked. 'I've sent Wells and the new student down to get theirs;

and there is half an hour before the prof. comes.'

They were discussing the advantages of moving Dolly Waters to the far end of the ward where a young woman with pneumonia had been admitted. 'It might do Dolly good to have someone cheerful to talk to her,' said Julia. 'Mrs Thorpe's a dear soul, but she's too ill to chat much, I think we'll move her . . .'

She looked up as the door, after the most peremptory of knocks, was thrust open, and the professor walked in. His 'Good morning' was so blighting that it seemed probable that the weather had affected him too. She said at once, quite forgetting that she was never going to offer him refreshment again: 'Would you like some coffee, sir?'

He fixed her with a black stare. 'No, Sister, I would not. I came in to see Dolly Waters, but perhaps it's not convenient?'

She disliked the silkiness of his voice but there was nothing she could do about it; open rebellion was out of the question. She put down her coffee mug and sailed to the door. 'We were discussing,' she informed him haughtily, 'whether it would be a good idea to move her next to Mary Perkins. Mary isn't very ill and might cheer up Dolly. Mrs Thorpe's a marvellous patient but I fancy she depresses Dolly.'

He had held the door wide for her to go through. 'I think that might be a sound idea, Sister.'

He spent some time with Dolly. It was remarkable thought Julia, standing on the other side of the bed watching him, that a man could make himself so disagreeable and within minutes switch on a charm and a warmth to put heart into the unhappiest patient. Which was the real man, she wondered. Only Martha would know that, she decided.

His examination finished, she accompanied him out of the ward and on the landing outside her office he paused long enough to remind her that he would be back to do his normal round in an hour's time.

He didn't smile but wished her a grave goodbye.

Back in her office Pat was sorting charts. 'I'll get some fresh coffee,' she said. 'I suppose he didn't want a cup now?'

'I didn't ask him,' said Julia with some heat. 'There's plenty of places in the hospital where he can get coffee if he wants it.'

Her staff nurse blinked in surprise. 'Why, Sister—was he cross?' She giggled. 'I've always rather fancied him, even when he's in a rage.'

'He's the most unfanciable man I know,' declared Julia. 'Let's have that coffee, shall we?'

Professor van der Wagema arrived on the dot, Dick Reed was with him and a handful of medical students and the round took a good deal longer than usual as the professor spent rather more time with each patient, listening with bland impatience to his pupils' halting answers to his questions. Julia felt sorry for the young men, standing there like schoolboys while he took them apart with a few biting phrases, though always out of earshot of the patients. It had always surprised her that to a man they liked him. They called him hard names behind his back, but let anyone say a word against him and they were immediately up in arms. And give him his due, his praise, though not given often, was worth something. He looked across at her as she was studying his face while he lectured, paused and smiled briefly at her.

She had been wrong—all these years she had been wrong; she didn't dislike him, she liked him, she suddenly understood why the bunch of young men standing around the bed liked him too. She would have to tell Nigel when she saw him, for he had never understood why she didn't share his respect for the professor. Not that she respected him, that was too strong a word. If anything she was vaguely sorry for him although she wasn't sure why—she had no reason to be, he had his Martha and his son and more than likely a most comfortable home to live in.

She smiled back at him, probably they would be at odds within the hour, but that didn't seem important. As it happened the rest of the round went smoothly and they drank their coffee, together with Dick Reed, in perfect harmony, the conversation exclusively about his patients.

Only as they were leaving did the professor observe, 'You go on holiday shortly, Sister?'

She nodded. 'Next week, sir. Staff Nurse Down will take over.'

'And for how long?'

'Ten days.'

He said surprisingly. 'Wellington goes with you, of course?'

'Of course.'

'And Longman?' His face was as bland as his voice and she mistrusted both. Besides, as one of the senior consultants at St Anne's he must be fully aware of the comings and goings of the registrars and senior housemen. He had no need to ask her, anyway she was sure that he already knew.

'If he is able to get a few days,' she said with vague sweetness.

Watching his broad back going down the corridor, she had to admit that although she was still prepared to like him, he could be awfully tiresome.

CHAPTER FOUR

THE day before Julia's holiday, she had a free evening. It had meant a rush from St Anne's to the flat to change rapidly, ram Wellington into his basket, pick up her case and nip down to the main street to find a taxi. It would have been nice if Nigel had been free to run her to Waterloo in his car, but he had had a long list in the afternoon and when she went off duty, theatre was still busy. She got into a cruising taxi, thankful to have found one so quickly and sat back with a sigh of relief, casting a quick look at the hospital as they passed it. There was a lot of traffic, she had barely ten minutes in which to catch her train but the queue for tickets was short and the Salisbury train was already at a nearby platform. She had paused to get a firmer grip on Wellington's basket when she saw Professor van der Wagema, coming towards her, and with him the same girl she had seen outside the cinema. He was the last person she had expected to see there and there was no way of avoiding him and his companion. She pinned a small smile on to her face and sped past them. The professor hadn't looked in the least surprised and Martha had glanced at her in a casual way without remembering her.

Julia was wrong there, the girl said at once, 'That's the redhead you spoke to the other evening.'

The professor took her arm to cross the street to where his car was parked. 'Sister Mitchell,' he agreed calmly. 'I'll drop you off if you don't mind—I've a round to do in the private wing.'

He didn't appear to notice his companion's pout.

Julia sprinting down the platform to find a seat, had hardly given the incident a second thought, it was only when the train was well under way and she sat, looking out into the autumn dusk, that she wondered what the professor was doing there—putting his wife on a train, meeting her? Perhaps she had been to see the boy at school. She looked very young to have a schoolboy for a son. She was quite lovely too. Julia sighed without knowing why, perhaps because it would be nice to have a son and be beautiful and have, too, the professor for a husband. She sat up straight at the thought, really, she was letting her imagination run away with her. She turned her thoughts to her holiday, dwelling happily on the days ahead. She would garden and go shopping for her mother and go riding and catch up on her reading, and when Nigel came for his free day, they would go for a long walk. There were miles of country in which to stretch their legs. She sighed again, this time with content, closed her eyes and dozed until they reached Salisbury.

The drive from the station was taken up with family gossip. Madge would be over to spend a day; Jason and Gregory were in their house football teams, and her mother had bought a new winter coat, Jane the donkey had had her hooves trimmed. Julia sitting with Wellington in his basket balanced on her knee, enjoyed every word of it.

Her mother welcomed her warmly and then stood back and gave her a good look. 'You're getting thin,' she declared, eyeing Julia's magnificent shape. 'Why?'

'Well, I didn't know that I was,' Julia found herself

making excuses. 'And anyway I'm huge, Mother—I feel like a mountain—you've no idea how slim most of the nurses are . . .'

Her mother, still what her father described with pride as a fine figure of a woman, gave her a tolerant smile. 'Well, it won't hurt you to put on a pound or two, darling, you'll lose it again when you get back to St Anne's.'

The hospital seemed another world by the end of her first day at home; the weather had looked kindly upon her and although it was chilly in the early mornings, it had been a lovely hazy day in which she had done almost nothing, she wandered off to her bed feeling relaxed, her head pleasantly empty of serious thoughts. And the moment she laid it on the pillow she was asleep, Wellington curled up tidily beside her.

She was in the kitchen the next morning, standing at the table, rolling pastry for the plum pie they were to have for lunch while her mother busied herself with something or other at the sink.

'Here's your father. There's someone with him. Heavens, was that—what a man! Julia do look. Well over six feet tall and enormous with it. He looks quite . . .' She broke off as Julia, nipping across to peer out of the window spoke.

'What on earth is he doing here?' she demanded a trifle wildly. 'It's his round . . .'

'Who is he?' asked Mrs Mitchell in a placid voice, just as though she hadn't guessed. 'And what round, darling?'

'Professor van der Wagema,' hissed Julia, 'his ward round.' She went back to the table and started slapping dabs of butter down on her pastry, if it didn't puff it would be too bad. From the brief glance she had allowed herself, the two gentlemen had been on the best of terms, deeply engrossed in conversation.

The kitchen door opened and her father and the professor came in.

'My dear,' said Mr Mitchell, 'here is Professor van der Wagema come to arrange for his son to have extra tuition in Latin. Luckily I can fit him in with the other boys I have . . .' He looked across at Julia. 'You know Julia, of course.'

The professor, shaking hands with Mrs Mitchell, agreed pleasantly that he did indeed. 'My hard-working right hand,' he murmured with a bland kindliness which set Julia's teeth on edge. 'And very deserving of a holiday.' He added politely, 'Cooking is your hobby?'

Before Julia could find her tongue her mother had answered. 'Oh, Julia's a splendid cook—she has a light hand with pastry too. You must stay to lunch, Professor?'

It annoyed Julia very much indeed when he accepted and was presently borne away by his host to sample a rather splendid dry sherry.

'What a charming man,' observed Mrs Mitchell, rapidly peeling more potatoes. 'How old is his son?'

'He's eleven years old apparently.'

'Any more children?' asked her mother chattily, 'and I wonder what kind of a wife he has.'

'I have no idea,' said Julia crossly and slapped her pastry down on to the fruit in the pie dish. Probably it would be as tough as leather and serve him right. She put the dish in the oven.

Her mother said,

'Do go and talk to the men love—only take that apron off first.'

'They'll be quite happy on their own, Mother, exchanging Latin tags and swapping Greek verbs. I'm going to lay the table and tidy myself.'

Her mother gently prodded the leg of lamb in the oven with her cooking fork. 'Well, well,' she said softly, and then: 'Oh, dear I do hope . . .' She closed the oven door gently and went upstairs to make sure that her appearance befitted the arrival of a visitor.

The table laid, Julia wandered up to her room, where she did her face, combed her hair into coppery neatness, wasted five minutes trying to make up her mind if she should change her dress, and deciding against it, went downstairs again.

'In your father's study, dear,' called her mother and after a moment's hesitation, she joined them. They were sitting round the fire with Maud, Muffin and Gyp with Wellington curled up between her paws, sitting tidily on the shabby hearth rug. The professor, sitting opposite her father, got to his feet, smiling a little. 'Will you sit here, Julia?'

'Don't get up, please.' She fetched a glass of sherry which her father had poured out for her and curled up in a corner of the sofa.

His smile widened a little as he sat down and resumed his talk with her father. Not Latin or Greek but education for boys; from time to time Mrs Mitchell and Julia were drawn into their talk and she had to admit that the professor was behaving beautifully; her father doubtless delighted to find someone as intelligent as himself, was enjoying himself, and her mother, she could see, was intrigued. Bursting to ask questions but unable to do so although probably she would discover a way to do that before long. She went to the kitchen presently to take a look at the lamb and was brought up shortly by her mother's voice as she went back into the study.

'And your wife, Professor? She lives in London too?' Mrs Mitchell's question was put so pleasantly that no one could take exception to it.

The professor looked over her shoulder to where Julia stood in the doorway. 'My wife died eight years ago, Mrs Mitchell. Nicholas and I are taken the greatest care of by my housekeeper. Martha has been with us for a long time now.'

Happily, Julia was unable to see her face, but the professor, watching her surprise, allowed himself a smile. 'Not,' he said smoothly, talking to Julia now, 'the young lady you met outside the cinema, Julia.'

'Well, I'm sorry,' said Mrs Mitchell, not feeling sorry at all, 'but how nice that you've someone to look after you so well. George, will you come and carve?' She swept her husband away. 'Finish your drink, Julia—perhaps the professor would like another . . .'

Julia scarcely heard her mother. After a moment alone with him in the quiet room, she said thoughtfully. 'How strange—I didn't know a thing about you all these years at St Anne's and then Mother asks a couple of questions . . .' She picked up her glass and finished her sherry. 'I won't tell anyone,' she promised him kindly.

'I would have said nothing if I had for one moment imagined that you would,' he told her crisply. 'You must have gathered by now that my private life is private.'

'Oh, indeed, yes. Tell me, Professor, why did you pick on Father to give your son extra lessons? Did you know that he was my father?'

He raised his eyebrows. 'Naturally I knew—you yourself mentioned it.'

She said with a frown, 'Oh, did I? I'm sure I never meant to . . .'

He laughed then. 'No, I imagine not. I shall be bringing him over to meet your father in a few days' time—on his half day, but if you do not care to meet me I will give you ample warning.'

She said coolly, 'Why shouldn't I want to meet you? After all, I'm always meeting you on the ward.'

'So you are, but in rather different circumstances. You tell me that you knew nothing about me in all the years we have been at St Anne's and now I realise that I knew nothing of you, Julia—the real you.' He smiled and she found herself smiling back at him. 'Making pastry and keeping an eye on the roast.' He paused. 'And I think that's the real you, isn't it?'

She answered him seriously: 'Yes, I think so. I like my work very much, I want to be a success at it, but there is so much more . . .'

He said quietly, 'I like my work too, but as you say there is so much more. And at the end of the day you know what that is, Julia? To love and be loved. Just that.'

She put her glass down carefully thinking what a pity it was that one couldn't ask any of the questions crowding into her head. Why was he talking to her like this? Was it an oblique reference to the lovely girl he had been with? Was he hinting that he was going to marry again? And why bother to tell her anyway? True, in the last few weeks they had become friends in a guarded way, but why should he suppose that she was interested in his love life? She was saved from wondering what to do next by her mother's cheerful voice, bidding them to come to lunch.

At that meal the professor's manner towards her was

so reminiscent of that of one of his more good-humoured rounds that Julia's splendid appetite was almost ruined by her bewilderment.

He left soon after lunch, promising to bring his son within the next few days and complimenting Mrs Mitchell on her delicious cooking. He gave Julia the briefest of nods and a careless, 'We shall see each other before long I have no doubt.'

'Well, of course we shall,' declared Julia sharply to his departing form, now out of earshot. 'Twice a week on the ward, not counting the odd visits when he takes a fit into his head . . .'

Her mother tucked an arm into hers, 'Such a nice man—but I expect he can be tiresome sometimes.'

Julia looked at her parent and encountered an innocent look. 'He's a very nice man,' she conceded, 'he likes his own way which I suppose is allowable seeing that he is an eminent physician, but he can be more sarcastic than you would ever believe, and he has a nasty temper. Just like me.'

Her mother smiled. 'How interesting darling. Let's do the washing up.'

Professor van der Wagema returned three days later, bringing his son with him. Julia was in the paddock behind the house, rubbing down Star while Jane edged backwards and forwards, not wanting to be left out. Julia was wearing an elderly corduroy skirt and a cotton sweater which had seen better days, and she hadn't bothered overmuch with her face or her hair, which she had tied back loosely and now it was very untidy. She looked up when she heard voices and her first wish to go somewhere and do her hair was swallowed up in indignation that the professor should take her unawares.

He then fetched up beside her and began to pull at Jane's ears. 'Hullo, Julia, I've brought Nicholas to meet you before he is introduced to your father! It's his half day.' He put a great arm on his son's shoulders. 'And Nicholas, this is Miss Julia Mitchell, my ward sister at St Anne's.'

Julia wiped a rather grubby hand on her skirt and held it out. 'Hullo, Nicholas, is my father waiting for you or would you like to take a look at Star and Jane?'

The boy was like his father, with the same direct dark gaze, and he had his smile too. 'May I?' He looked up at his father who said casually, 'I don't see why not, I have to have a talk with Mr Mitchell, I might just as well have it now as later if he finds that convenient. Ten minutes?'

Julia and Nicholas nodded in unison. 'Do you ride?' she asked the boy. He nodded. 'Oh, yes—Father and I go riding early in the mornings when we're in the country. I've a pony of my own. I like Jane.'

'She's a sweetie, isn't she? She doesn't do much now, though, she's quite elderly, but she loves to be with Star.' She thrust her hand into a pocket. 'Here, give her this carrot, will you and here is some sugar for Star. We'd better go to the house I think.'

They stroked the animals' noses, bade them be good and started back across the paddock. 'Are you coming here for your tuition or having it at school?' asked Julia.

'I'm to have it at school,' he told her, 'but Mr Mitchell said that I could come over on my half days if I liked and have a lesson then.'

'That'll be nice—other boys have done that from time to time. I expect you are looking forward to the holidays?'

'Rather, only Father has to work most days, but when he is free we go out—that's when we are in London.'

Julia's curiosity got the better of her. 'You said you had a pony in the country . . .'

'I have, we've got a cottage just outside Winchester, when Father can get away, we go there with Martha— I like it much better than London.'

'You like school?'

'Oh, yes. I shall be a doctor when I grow up, of course.'

'Well, yes . . . We'll go in through the kitchen, then we can wipe our feet.'

She ushered him into the hall and poked her head round the study door. 'I've brought Nicholas—shall he come in?'

Her father peered over his glasses. 'Yes, my dear. You're rather untidy, Julia.'

'Star needed his hooves seen to.' She didn't look at the professor, although she was very conscious of him watching her. 'Here's Nicholas.'

She went upstairs and met her mother coming down. 'Darling, your hair.' Her parent paused on the top step. 'They'll stay to tea,' she suggested.

Julia tugged off her hair ribbon. 'I've no idea. Is Nicholas to have a first lesson today? If so you'll have to entertain the professor.'

'I'll get the tea,' observed her mother and gave her a limpid look. 'You can entertain him, after all you must have a great deal to talk about; patients and so forth . . .'

'Mother,' began Julia and then laughed. 'Well, he'll have to entertain himself until I get down.'

She didn't hurry. She put on a silk shirt blouse and

a tweed skirt and sat down before her dressing table to make up her face carefully and brush her hair into a loose roll. She secured the last pin, took a keen look at her reflection and then went downstairs. There was no sign of the professor, either in the sitting room or the dining room; she could hear the faint drone of voices coming from her father's study, perhaps he was there. She went along to the kitchen and opened the door. 'He's gone,' she began and saw him, hands in his pockets, leaning against the old-fashioned dresser, watching her mother cut up one of her seed cakes.

'No, he's here,' observed the professor at his most urbane. 'There's something about a kitchen which makes for conviviality.' He eyed her splendid proportions with an appreciative eye, and Julia, always so calm and collected, suddenly felt awkward.

'Oh, indeed? By the same token there's something about a hospital ward which makes for sarcasm and ill humour.'

He allowed himself the faintest of smiles, and she said quickly, 'I wouldn't dare to say that on the ward.'

'I should hope not, indeed, but feel free to speak your own mind in your own home, Julia.'

'Shall we have tea?' interposed Mrs Mitchell, 'you can argue so much more comfortably sitting round a table. Be a dear and carry in the tray, will you, Professor? Julia, you bring that plate of scones, I dare say those two will be hungry after all that Latin.'

The professor laughed and after a minute, so did Julia. She didn't know why he was amused; she had laughed at the very idea of the professor being told to carry the tray, something she suspected he seldom did in his own home.

Mr Mitchell, still muttering Latin tags under his

breath, and Nicholas looking pleased with himself, joined them round the table; Mrs Mitchell had always made a point of setting a good old-fashioned tea before her family, even when the boys weren't home, it made a pleasant break in the late afternoon and still left a leisurely evening before supper.

Nicholas sitting beside Julia at the large round table, eyed the food with pleasure and needed no urging to make a good tea. And his father, Julia noticed, ate equally heartily. Of course, he was a very large man and perhaps he hadn't had much lunch . . .

The talk was light hearted and general and everyone joined in. Nicholas had nice manners and although he was a little shy, held his own well enough when called upon to take his share in the conversation. They sat over the leisurely meal until the professor looked at his watch.

'I am reluctant to say that we must go—I have to hand Nicky over before half-past seven, and it will take us twenty minutes or so to drive back.'

They all went into the hall and Nicholas hung back to say to Julia, 'I hope I may come again, I like it here and I like you.'

'Why thank you, Nicholas.' She was touched by his friendly overture, 'I expect we'll see each other again—I'm on holiday for another week.'

The professor wasn't a man to hang around saying endless goodbyes. He shook hands, complimented Mrs Mitchell on her delicious cakes, thanked Mr Mitchell for his kindness in seeing Nicholas, waited while the boy made his own polite farewells and ushered him out to the car, pausing only a moment to mutter *'Haec olim meminisse juvabit'* into her surprised ear.

'And what did that mean?' she asked her father, watching the big car slide away down the lane.

'It will be a joy to us to recall this some day.' Her father added in some satisfaction, 'A scholar—let us hope that Nicholas takes after him.'

Julia wasn't listening. 'Now why on earth should he say that?' she asked herself and followed her mother indoors. Her mother who had listened with interest, didn't feel called upon to answer her.

Nigel came for the weekend, driving himself down; he looked tired and vaguely worried and Julia guessed that he had had a busy time at the hospital. She took him out into the garden to a sheltered sunny corner and carried out the coffee tray. 'Mother and Father have gone into Salisbury but they'll be back for lunch.'

She had hoped that he would have wanted to discuss their future but she squashed that idea at once; he wasn't in the mood. She plied him with coffee and her mother's cake and listened with a sympathetic ear to his account of the week's work, commenting suitably when he paused for breath. But presently he enquired, 'And you? What have you been doing, Julia?'

'Oh, rides on old Star and then helping Mother and doing a bit of gardening.' For some reason she didn't want to tell him about the professor's visit; her father would almost certainly mention it anyway.

She went in presently to get lunch, leaving him in the sunshine. But when Mr and Mrs Mitchell returned he came indoors and they all sat around talking, plying him with questions about his new job.

'So now you can think about getting married,' declared Mrs Mitchell.

'Well, perhaps,' he smiled at her indulgently. 'I

must find my feet first and we ought to wait for an opening for Julia . . . There are a couple of posts vacant in the early summer.'

Mrs Mitchell said nothing and he went on defensively, 'We thought that she could go on working for a time. She'd be bored alone all day, anyway.'

'I was never bored,' declared Mrs Mitchell sharply, 'but then I had the housework to do and the shopping and then the children. One is never bored with children—frustrated—ill-tempered, tired to death with them, but never bored.'

Julia thought it prudent to go into the kitchen and make the salad. She didn't want to take part in the argument, however reasonably it would be conducted; she had a feeling that she might be unreasonable if someone asked her what she felt about it.

Over lunch Mr Mitchell mentioned the professor's visit.

'Well, I'll be damned,' said Nigel, 'who would have thought it? How very domestic too . . .'

'You're not to tell anyone,' said Julia firmly. 'He's—he's a very private person and I don't think he'd want the whole of St Anne's to know that he's been married and that he has a son.'

'Why ever not?' Nigel was laughing at her.

'Father told you because you're almost family—you should respect his confidence.' She added almost pleadingly. 'Please promise you won't tell anyone, Nigel?'

He shrugged. 'Okay—if it makes you happy. And that's funny coming from you—you spend your time biting each other's heads off.'

'I don't see that that has anything to do with it. He's my boss and I must be loyal to him, you must see that.'

'All right, although I think you're taking things too seriously. What's the boy like?'

'Eleven years old. Rather like his father . . .'

'Clever too,' put in her father. 'Sharp as a needle. I'm interested to see how he gets on with the other boys when I go next week.'

Nigel had lost interest. He began to talk about Bristol again and Julia, relieved to have skimmed over the little matter of the professor's visit, encouraged him.

The weekend went quickly. Nigel didn't ride, but they went for long walks and to church on Sunday. The vicar, standing at the door after the service beamed at them. 'And when are we to have the wedding?' he asked jovially.

It was Nigel who answered him: 'Not just yet, Vicar. Perhaps in the early summer.'

The vicar looked rather surprised, then laughed uncertainly. 'Just so—"Marry in haste . . ." I am always cautioning young people of this parish.'

Julia smiled at him because he was doing his best. She wanted to remind him that neither she nor Nigel were young people but that would have been unkind. She said cheerfully, 'A summer wedding is the nicest I think.'

Nigel went back on Sunday evening and they still hadn't talked much about the future. She had tried but each time he had changed the subject and she wasn't sure if it had been intentional. Perhaps when she got back to the hospital they would have a quiet evening in her flat and she would try and make him see her point of view.

They waved him away from the porch and Julia found herself thinking of the professor's departure.

One day, she promised herself, when he was in a good mood, she would ask him what he had meant, quoting that Latin tag to her.

It seemed very quiet on Monday with Nigel gone and her father away at the two prep schools he visited. He wouldn't be home until the evening for they were some miles away. She and her mother made short work of the chores, crammed the washing machine and set it going and sat down to drink their coffee.

Her mother sipped reflectively. 'Darling, don't think I'm prying but I can't quite understand why Nigel is so keen on you working once you're married, and why wait until next summer? He's got the job and a place to live and neither of you are ... What I mean is, you're both sensible enough to manage very well.'

Julia stirred her coffee for the second time. 'I don't quite understand either, Mother.' She sounded forlorn. 'I—I don't seem able to make Nigel understand that I'm not getting any younger. Even if we married now . . .' She gave a rueful little laugh. 'I'll be a very elderly Mum. Perhaps he hasn't thought about that; when I get back we must have a talk and get things straight.'

'Yes, dear. What do his people think about it I wonder?'

'I've no idea.' Julia gave her mother a direct look, her eyes very green. 'I'll have to find that out, won't I?'

'It's not really anyone's business but yours, darling. Do we want to do anything today?'

'Let's be lazy. I thought I'd take Star for a good trot tomorrow; he's getting too fat. I'll go down and see to the pair of them now, shall I?'

The day was peaceful. It was still fine but getting
chilly now, Julia pottered contentedly until it was time
to help her mother with supper and when her father
came home they sat around the log fire over drinks,
discussing their day. 'I've asked that boy of Professor
van der Wagema's over for a while at half term,' Mr
Mitchell told his wife. 'His father's working it seems
and there is no point him going home to a more or less
empty house. He jumped at the idea—wanted to know
if he could ride Star?' He turned to Julia. 'A pity you
won't be here, Julia; we could borrow Ben Stratton's
mare and you and Nicholas could have a good ride
together.'

'When is his half term?' she asked idly. And when
he told her, 'That's my weekend, I'm almost sure. I'll
come home of you like,' she grinned. 'In fact I'll come
home whether you like it or not; it'll be nice to get
away from St Anne's for a couple of days.'

'Could Nigel get free too?' asked her mother.

'He'll be in Bristol. That's the weekend he starts
there.'

She passed her plate for a second helping. 'He plans
to go to his parents on the Saturday and Sunday and
report for work on Sunday evening ready for Monday
morning.'

'Oh, well, then that fits in beautifully, love, you'll
be glad to have something to do. You're bound to miss
him . . .'

Julia nodded. The prospect of long winter evenings
on her own wasn't inviting; she could always spend
them with her friends, of course, but one couldn't go
to the cinema or the theatre on every free evening.
There would be letters to write of course, and then
Wellington for company and the odd weekend spent

with friends who had married. She should be content, but she wasn't, it worried her a bit.

They breakfasted early so that her father could go into Salisbury to take a class, and the housework done, Julia saddled Star and rode at a leisurely pace along the country lanes and bridle paths. Because it was overcast and chilly she had donned slacks and an old, out-at-elbows sweater and tied a bright scarf over her red head, but once she had urged the pony to a smarter pace, she glowed with warmth, so that her cheeks were a bright pink and her hair became loose under the scarf and escaped in thick waving tresses. They turned for home at last, Star ambling the last mile, glad to get back to his stall and Jane, but determined not to hurry too much.

He gave a happy little snort as Julia swung herself out of the saddle and Jane replied. She led him inside the old barn he shared with the donkey and then stopped suddenly. The professor was sitting comfortably on a truss of hay against one wall with Jane as close as she could get while he rubbed her ears.

'Well,' said Julia, letting out a held breath, 'you could have coughed or something—I had the fright of my life.'

'Do I frighten you, Julia?' And then, in quite a different voice, 'I was on my way back from seeing Nicky and I called in to see if I could give you a lift back—you return on Friday, don't you? I shall be passing about tea time if that suits you?'

He had got off the hay and was unsaddling Star in a businesslike way.

'Well, thank you, I'd be glad of a lift, it would help as it would save Father having to drive me in to Salisbury, and tea time would be just right.' She eyed his elegant clothes. 'Look—I'll do this, you'll get in a mess and that's a good suit. Has mother asked you to stay for lunch?'

The professor's mouth twitched at its corners. 'Yes, but I must refuse her kind offer, I have to get back as soon as possible.'

She was surprised to feel disappointment. 'Oh, well—I'll walk with you to the house.'

'No need. I will tell your mother you are back—ten minutes?'

'Yes, and many thanks for the offer of a lift. It—it was kind of you to think of it.'

He said gravely, 'Occasionally I give way to these generous impulses. Till Friday.'

She watched him walk away. Even from the back he looked distinguished.

Friday came too soon as the last day of a holiday always does. Julia went for a last early morning ride, groomed Star and Jane, ate the lunch her mother had been at such pains to cook for her, and went away to pack and get herself dressed. An hour later she descended, looking quite different in a knitted jacket and skirt and a tucked silk blouse, all in a soft grey which did full justice to her hair, now very neatly coiled at the back of her head. She hadn't bothered overmuch with make-up while she had been at home, but now she had done her face with great care.

'Smashing,' declared her mother. 'You're wearing the Gucci shoes.'

'Well, I thought I might as well.' The whole outfit looked what her mother called vogue-ish and she said so, carefully not betraying her interest in her daughter's reasons for taking such pains. Mrs Mitchell, who had taken to the professor and had a strong romantic streak, wondered what complications lay ahead.

'I'm sure the professor will have a cup of tea,' she observed comfortably. 'I've made some cress sandwiches, and there's that chocolate cake you made yesterday.'

Professor van der Wagema, when he came, professed himself delighted to stay for tea. He had greeted his hostess with a charm which started off the romantic thoughts once more, said hullo in a casual way to Julia and went to shake Mr Mitchell by the hand, that gentleman having just come in from his school visits.

Tea was a pleasant meal but they didn't linger over it. They were at the door saying their goodbyes when Mrs Mitchell asked, 'When will you be home again, darling?'

Julia was deliberately vague. 'I'm not sure, Mother—I'll give you a ring—it won't be for a couple of weeks, anyway.' She gave her parent a final kiss and got into the Rolls, feeling for once that she was dressed in a style befitting its subdued luxury. The professor put her case in the boot, Wellington in his basket on the back seat, and then got in beside her.

'You don't mind getting back early?' He wanted to know as he took the road to Salisbury. 'I've a date this evening and I must get home to change.'

That horrible girl, thought Julia and said airily, 'It suits me very well: Nigel's free this evening and we'll have an hour or two together.'

This wasn't really true and she didn't know when he was free but she didn't suppose that her companion knew either and bringing him into the conversation put, she considered, the professor nicely in his place. She felt quite pleased with herself for having been so ready with an answer and the professor, well aware that Mr Longman was on duty until midnight, saw no reason to disabuse her. He glanced sideways at her. 'You look quite different out of uniform, Julia.' His voice was pleasant and rather cool and she answered him just as coolly.

'Do I? I expect we all do—nurses you know.'

They were through Salisbury before she broke the silence. 'How is Nicholas?'

'Happy. He's enjoying his extra lessons. And he's got into the house rugger team.'

'Oh, good for him. Jason and Gregory are in different houses, of course, but Jason's in the school team and Greg's in his house team this term.'

'A common talking point if the three of them should ever meet,' commented the professor.

They didn't at any time talk much and not a word about the ward or St Anne's. It was already dusk turning rapidly to dark by the time he drew up outside the flat. Julia thanked him for her lift and put out a hand to open the door. His hand came down over hers. 'I'll bring up your case,' he told her, 'and stay where you are.'

He got out and opened her door, fetched Wellington's basket, ushered her on to the pavement and fetched her case.

'There's no need,' protested Julia. 'You'll be too late for your date.'

'Time enough.' He sounded casual as he opened the shabby street door and followed her upstairs.

The flat looked poky when she opened her door. She went straight to the window and opened it, letting in much-needed air redolent of petrol fumes and the fish and chip shop on the corner.

'Oh dear.' She smiled at him ruefully, 'after all that fresh air and lovely silence. I'll have to get used to it again . . .'

'Not for long, perhaps. The country around Bristol is quite charming and rural.'

She said wistfully, 'But we shall have to live in a flat attached to the hospital. It'll be more convenient.'

He had put down her case and closed the door and when she opened Wellington's basket he got out at once and went sniffing round the room. 'He's looking for Gyp,' said Julia, 'they formed a lasting friendship.'

She looked uncertainly at the professor, looming there in the middle of the room. 'Don't let me keep you, you've been most kind and I am grateful.'

He stared back at her. 'Has it struck you that the tone of our conversation has altered during the past few weeks? So polite, almost if I might say so, friendly. We must do our best to correct that, mustn't we? Our years of cut and thrust have become a habit, haven't they?'

She kept her eyes on him. She didn't think that he was serious, but one could never tell. She said cautiously, 'If you say so, Professor.'

She sidled to the door, ready to usher him out. 'Ah, speed the parting guest,' observed the professor in what she always thought of as his nasty voice.

She returned kindly, 'Oh, no—I was thinking of your date.'

He took the door handle from her, towering over her and leaving precious little room for the pair of them in the doorway. He said softly, 'I hope that you dressed yourself to kill on my account, Julia,' and bent and kissed her. He was half way down the first flight of stairs before she could get her breath and then it was only a squeak.

CHAPTER FIVE

WITHIN half an hour of being back on the ward the next morning, it was as if Julia had never been away; most of the patients were still there. Medical patients were much slower to recover than those in the surgical wards, but there were half-a-dozen new faces to be smiled at and talked to, their charts examined and their notes carefully read.

Mrs Collins had gone, rather to her surprise and when she asked Pat about her, her staff nurse said eagerly, 'Oh, Sister such a piece of luck, her niece heard from someone she knew who wanted help in the house—not housework, mind you—mending and polishing silver and that kind of thing, just right for Mrs Collins, she was offered a bed-sitting room and promised that she should see her doctor regularly. Wasn't that super? Heaven knows what would have happened to the old dear ... The niece simply couldn't have her, she decided—it would have meant a geriatric ward for ever and ever.'

'What a mercy this turned up, then. I wonder who it was? I must find out. Did the social worker know about it? I mean the details?'

Pat nodded, 'Oh, yes! She said she'd see you when you got back.' She added, 'As a matter of fact, she's on holiday for a week.'

'Oh, lord that means we'll have that beady eyed Miss Trump doing her work. I'll wait until she's back. Now let's get through these notes ...'

The day was long but busy and at the end of it, she had the evening with Nigel. They went back to the flat and she cooked supper for them both while he described a tricky splenectomy he'd done that afternoon. Over their coffee he asked, 'Did you have a good journey back?'

'A nice easy one. Professor van der Wagema gave me a lift, he'd been to see his son.'

'It must have been early in the evening—he came in to see a patient just before midnight, all rigged out in a black tie. One of the housemen saw him in his car during the week with a smashing blonde.'

He didn't wait for Julia's answer. 'I'm going home in a couple of weeks' time—Saturday and come back Sunday evening—coming with me?'

Julia thrust the picture of the professor and the ravishing blonde to the back of her mind. 'I'd love to. Give me the dates sometime, will you, so that I can fit in with Pat. It's her weekend but I know she wants days off in the middle of the week. Couldn't be better.'

When Nigel had gone she washed up and got ready for bed. She wasn't keen to spend the weekend with his family, but common sense told her that since she was going to be their daughter-in-law in the not too distant future, she had better start getting to know them better. The matter occupied her thoughts until she was in bed, with Wellington purring beside her, but the last thing she thought of, funnily enough, before she slept was Professor van der Wagema and the fair beauty.

'I only hope she is kind to Nicholas,' she observed to Wellington as she closed her eyes.

She didn't meet the professor again until three days later, when he came to do his customary ward round.

She saw at once that he was in one of his austere moods; coldly polite with his: 'Sister Mitchell this and Sister Mitchell that.' With his patients he was—as she had to admit—kind and sympathetic, showing no sign of impatience with the more garrulous ladies and taking time to instil some of his own assurance into Mrs Thorpe who was making no progress at all. And afterwards in her office while they drank their coffee, he confined the conversation to his patients, talking for the most part to Dick Reed. She found it hard, almost impossible to believe that this was the man who had kissed her only a few days ago. Of course, he had meant nothing by it; she was no green girl to believe otherwise, all the same, did he have to be very formal with her? Perhaps he felt awkward, she had had a few qualms about meeting him but she was a sensible woman and didn't allow them to become serious, so why should he have any? He put out a hand without looking at her and she put a pen into it. As he bent to sign the form Dick had given him she had time to look at him. He was undoubtedly good looking and very distinguished. There was a sprinkling of grey in his dark hair and she thought how unfair it was that a man approaching forty-two could still attract admiring glances from the girls, while a woman of thirty worried herself sick at the mere thought of being thirty-one. He looked up suddenly and caught her eyes upon him. They stared at each other for a few seconds while the colour crept slowly into her cheeks. He smiled then before turning to Dick to query something. It gave her cheeks the chance to cool while she reflected in a muddled way that it was a good thing that Nigel was free that evening and would be coming round to the flat for supper.

Not a successful evening, as it turned out. Nigel had had a bad day and it took him a long time to get it off his chest and by the time she had offered sympathy and they had had supper the evening was over. He could have stayed later of course, but he didn't want to; she kissed him good night with extra warmth but he didn't respond, only reminded her that he had a heavy list in the morning and she mustn't expect to see him.

Indeed she saw very little of him for the next week or ten days although they had met for long enough to arrange to go to his parents on the following weekend. And the weekend after that, she remembered forlornly, he would be leaving for Bristol.

She had gone home just for a day and wished for longer there to enjoy the autumn countryside and was overjoyed to find that Pat didn't want the weekend due to her, which meant that Julia could have the weekend that Nigel was due to leave for Bristol. She had told him that, and waited to see if he would ask her to go with him, but since he didn't she would go home; it would make their parting less painful.

But they still had their weekend together with his parents. They drove down early on the Saturday morning leaving dull cloudy weather behind them and arriving at his home in bright sunshine.

Mr and Mrs Longman greeted her pleasantly but without warmth; she wasn't sure why they didn't welcome her into the family; after all, she would soon be a member of it. They were always meticulously polite, thoughtful of her comfort but she was always a guest, never one of them. She handed Mrs Longman the flowers she had brought with her, offered a cheek to Mr Longman and following Nigel went indoors.

The main topic of conversation of course, was Nigel's new job although they weren't particularly interested in her and Nigel's future together. A flat, they said, how nice, you can set up house later, but of course there's no hurry, Nigel must get himself established first; Julia had a good job, hadn't she? And they could meet whenever they could arrange weekends ... Julia agreed, because she could see it wouldn't help matters if she did otherwise. Later, perhaps, she would be able to get Nigel on his own and make a few definite plans.

Easier said than done—family friends came after dinner that evening and on Sunday morning they all went to church before sitting down to Sunday lunch, a leisurely meal. Julia's hopes for a walk with Nigel afterwards were shattered by his mother's insistence that Julia should be shown a family photo album, the contents of which were explained in great detail to her, so that by the time they had reached its end, it was time for tea. And after tea they were to drive back to London.

In the car at last, Julia heaved a quiet sigh; at least they had an hour or two in each other's company. She began at once, wasting no time, 'Nigel—your mother and father—they do know that we want to get married? Sometimes it would appear to me that they don't take it seriously; I feel that I don't belong ...'

'My dear girl—after all, they don't know you very well, do they? I mean, you've been home, what—half a dozen times. I'm sure that they like you but it'll take them a little while to accept you. Once I'm at Bristol you must try and visit them more often.'

He dismissed the whole thing with a good-natured laugh. 'You want too much from people, Julia, you can't expect everything to be just as you want it. You must come down again in a few weeks and you can all come over and see me at the hospital; I might even manage a couple of days off . . .'

'That will be nice,' observed Julia quietly. Only her eyes betrayed her disappointment, unease, and unhappiness, and it was too dark for anyone to see their green glitter.

It was an uneasy week, not helped in the least by a sudden influx of patients, ill enough to keep her busy while she was on duty and too tired when she got off to think very much about her own affairs. Nigel was busy too, which meant that they only had two evenings together, and even their final dinner before he left St Anne's had to be shelved at the last moment because of a run of emergencies in theatre with which he had to deal.

By Friday evening Julia was miserably unhappy, with luck Nigel might manage half an hour with her when he had finished in the theatre, too late for her to cook supper for the pair of them and far too late to have the dinner they had planned at their favourite restaurant. It would have to be a drink and something in a basket at the nearest pub, not the most romantic of places in which to bid each other a temporary goodbye. All the same, she went back to the flat, saw to Wellington's supper, packed an overnight bag ready to leave the next morning for home, and changed into a pretty dress. She looked every day of her thirty years, she decided, studying her tired face in the mirror, and proceeded to make it up with extra care. She took pains with her hair too and found a pair of low-heeled shoes so that her tired feet wouldn't ache.

They had just sent down the last case; the night

porter, just come on duty, obligingly told her and ten minutes later Nigel joined her in the entrance hall. 'Lord, what a way to finish,' he began ruefully, 'I'm glad I've a couple of days' peace and quiet at home before I start at Bristol.'

Julia agreed with him although the thought crossed her mind that they could have spent the weekend together only he didn't seem to have thought about that. They walked the short distance to the 'Mug and Thistle' and sat, she with a glass of wine, he with a pint of old and mild, a plate of sandwiches between them. It would be closing time in less than an hour and Julia, listening to him describing the tricky perforation he had dealt with that evening, wondered unhappily if that was all they were to talk about. After all, they wouldn't be seeing each other for some time and even if they were seldom together at St Anne's, at least they were under the same roof. Then she said abruptly, 'I shall miss you, Nigel.'

He stopped abruptly in mid-sentence, frowning: 'Darling, you aren't listening, I was describing this appendix . . .'

'Well, will you miss me?' persisted Julia.

'Of course I shall, what a silly question. But don't expect a lot of letters darling; I'll give you a ring whenever I can—you'd better not ring me until I give you a number . . .' He smiled at her. 'I'm damned lucky to get this job, Julia—it's a real stroke of luck.'

She exerted herself to be cheerful and interested. After all, Bristol wasn't all that far away and they would be able to fix their holidays together, even weekends. Only she was going to be lonely and she longed to tell him that, but how could she when she suspected that he wasn't going to be lonely himself?

He might love her but she wasn't the be all and end all of everything for him; she would be there, in the background, waiting for him when he was ready to settle down, but he wasn't the man to fling everything to the four winds of heaven for love of her. She doubted if there were such a man.

They walked back to the hospital presently and bade each other goodbye. A totally unsatisfactory exercise from Julia's point of view. She walked quickly back to the flat, feeling let down and miserable again. It had been a beastly week, she reflected, putting the key in her door and stooping to scoop up Wellington for a cuddle. The ward had been busy, which would account for her feeling so sorry for herself and over and above that, Professor van der Wagema had been at his most aloof and prickly. There had been no pleasing him and she had been hard put to it to present her usual serene front before his intent dark gaze.

It was quite unlike her to cry herself to sleep, but presently she did just that.

She caught an early morning train, doing her best to swamp her unhappy feelings in the bustle of getting to the station with Wellington and her overnight bag. Her father was waiting for her at Salisbury, and being somewhat absent minded, enquired of her if Nigel would be joining her later before the black look on her pale lovely face finally reminded him, and he begged pardon hurriedly and went on in a rush, 'Well, we've a guest for the weekend, my dear—Nicholas—it's his half term and his father had to attend some seminar or other which would have meant him staying at school, so I brought him back with me yesterday. He's as happy as a sandboy, whatever that may mean, riding Star and grooming Jane. A nice lad . . .'

YOUR DREAMS CAN COME TRUE
HARLEQUIN
FIRST•CLASS
Sweepstakes
AIR FRANCE
Enter and you can win a
♦ ROLLS-ROYCE™ ♦ TRIP TO PARIS ♦ MINK COAT

'O EXPERIENCE A WORLD OF ROMANCE.

How to Enter Sweepstakes & How to get 4 FREE BOOKS, A FREE TOTE BAG and A BONUS MYSTERY GIFT.

1. Check ONLY ONE OPTION BELOW.
2. Detach Official Entry Form and affix proper postage.
3. Mail Sweepstakes Entry Form before the deadline date in the rules.

H·A·R·L·E·Q·U·I·N
FIRST·CLASS
Sweepstakes

OFFICIAL ENTRY FORM

Check one:

☐ Yes. Enter me in the Harlequin First Class Sweepstakes and send me 4 FREE HARLEQUIN ROMANCE® novels plus a FREE Tote Bag and a BONUS Mystery Gift. Then send me 6 brand new HARLEQUIN ROMANCE® novels every month as they come off the presses. Bill me at the low price of $1.65 each (a savings of $0.30 off the retail price). There are no shipping, handling or other hidden charges. I understand that the 4 Free Books, Tote Bag and Mystery Gift are mine to keep with no obligation to buy.

☐ No. I don't want to receive the Four Free HARLEQUIN ROMANCE® novels, a Free Tote Bag and a Bonus Gift. However, I do wish to enter the sweepstakes. Please notify me if I win.

116–CIR–EAXR

See back of book for official rules and regulations.
Detach, affix postage and mail Official Entry Form today!

FIRST NAME_____ LAST NAME_____
(Please Print)

ADDRESS_____ APT._____

CITY_____

PROV./STATE_____ POSTAL CODE/ZIP_____
"Subscription Offer limited to one per household and not valid to current Harlequin Romance® subscribers. Prices subject to change."

ENTER THE H•A•R•L•E•Q•U•I•N
FIRST•CLASS *Sweepstakes*

Detach, Affix Postage and Mail Today!

Harlequin First Class Sweepstakes
P.O. Box 52010
Phoenix, AZ 85072-9987

Julia received this piece of news calmly and upon reflection decided that it would be rather nice to have company. 'We could ride down the valley,' she suggested, 'I'll 'phone the riding school and borrow Juno . . .'

Her father looked pleased. 'Well, my dear, I took it upon myself to do that—she's in the paddock, waiting for you.'

'Super, thank you, Father. We might get a ride in before lunch.'

'That's what your mother thought.' They were out of the city now, driving along the familiar road with home barely a couple of miles away. She was feeling better already; her life at St Anne's was dropping away into a vague other world she wouldn't allow herself to think about until Monday morning; she wouldn't think about Nigel either. He would 'phone her as soon as he could and everything would be just as it used to be.

The house looked beautifully peaceful in the pale autumn sunshine, there were still roses in the garden and the lawn was covered in leaves. Julia ran indoors to be greeted by her mother and after a minute, a rather shy Nicholas.

'I won't be in the way?' he wanted to know anxiously, 'Mr Mitchell said you wouldn't mind if I rode Star.'

'I think it's lovely that you are here,' said Julia warmly. 'Just give me time to settle Wellington and have some coffee and get into some slacks and we'll be off. There are almost two hours before lunch.'

The boy smiled at her and she was reminded sharply of his father, whose smile, though rare, was charming. 'I like you,' he told her gravely.

'And I like you. Will you see to Wellington, while I have coffee and change?'

'I've a little cat and Father has a dog at home,' he told her seriously. 'While I'm at school he looks after Minou for me. She's a moggy, like Wellington.'

'The very best kind of cat,' Julia assured him, swallowing coffee and gobbling the slice of cake her mother had cut for her.

Ten minutes later she swung herself on to Juno and, with Nicholas urging Star to exert himself, they took the bridle path going towards Broad Chalke. They turned off presently to ride slowly along by the river while Nicholas told her about his school.

'You're happy there?' asked Julia and hoped that he was, he was a dear boy and she liked him better every minute.

'Oh, yes, I'll go to a public school when I'm old enough and then I'll go to Holland and study to be a doctor.'

Julia turned to look at him in surprise. 'Holland, but why?'

'Father studied at Leiden, so I shall too, then I'll come back here and take an English degree or perhaps a Scottish one.'

'But won't it be difficult for you studying in a different language?'

'No, you see I speak Dutch with Father, and we go to my grandmother's house quite often. It's not her house really, it's father's but she lives in it.'

Julia blinked. 'Oh, I see.' She slowed Juno down so that Star's portly form could keep up with her. 'Well, it's nice to have your future settled.' Which remark reminded her that it would be nice to have her own future settled as neatly.

They had gone out into a lane once more, high banked and narrow, and they went into single file. 'We'll turn off at the crossroads,' said Julia, 'that should get us back in nice time for lunch.'

The crossroads were round the next bend and waiting for them there was the professor. Julia reined in sharply.

She said, a little breathless. 'Oh, hullo—I thought you were at some seminar or other.'

Nicholas had urged Star alongside his father's great horse, Goliath, from the same stables as Juno, a mettlesome beast, most suitable for a man of his size. 'Father, what a lovely surprise—didn't you have to go after all?'

'I cried off.' The professor put a large hand on the boy's shoulder. 'It wasn't absolutely essential that I went and I have to go to Groningen very shortly anyway.' He looked across to where Julia was sitting very still on Juno. 'May I join you? Are you on the way back?'

'Well, yes, Mother said lunch at one o'clock. I expect she'll ask you to stay unless you have other plans?'

'None. And I'd like ten minutes' talk with Mr Mitchell afterwards if he can spare the time?'

He turned Goliath and they ambled down the lane running between grassland sloping away to hills and with nothing ahead of them in sight. 'Your weekend, Julia?' enquired the professor.

She had a strong suspicion that he knew that already. Her 'Yes,' was a little pettish.

'Longman's gone?' The question was carelessly put.

'Yes,' said Julia again, and then because she didn't want to be ungracious, 'He went today and he starts

work on Monday.' And since it seemed to her that he
would ask the inevitable question: 'He has gone to stay
with his parents . . .'

But beyond a kind of rumble and a lift of the
eyebrows, the professor had nothing to say to this.
They rode in silence for a while until Nicholas said
eagerly, 'You're staying, Father? Don't you have to go
back to London?'

'No, Nicky, I don't have to go back until tomorrow
evening, but if you'd like to go home we'll go after
lunch . . .'

'I'd rather stay, Father. You see I can ride all I want
here and there's Julia to talk to.'

'That's fine, Nicky. I'll be at the pub at Broad
Chalke.'

They rode in silence for a little. Julia spoke at last:
'There's heaps of room at home, I'm sure Mother will
be glad to put you up, Professor, since Nicholas is
staying with us.' She sounded reluctant.

He turned a bland face to her. 'How very kind.' His
voice was a nice mixture of surprise, pleasure and
nicely balanced reluctance, 'But I couldn't possibly
impose upon her . . .'

Julia had her mouth open ready to tell him that in
that case she was sure her mother would understand,
but Nicholas spoke before she could get the words out.
'Smashing! Father we can ride before breakfast . . .'

The professor glanced at Julia, a little smile
twitching the corners of his mouth, for all the world as
though he had known what she had been going to say.

'In that case we must hope for Mrs Mitchell's
kindness, Nicky.'

A foregone conclusion. Mrs Mitchell greeted him
with pleasure, urged him to stay to lunch and when

Nicholas told her that his father was putting up in Broad Chalke said instantly, 'Of course you must stay here, Professor—we shall all love to have you, shan't we Julia? We've room enough now the boys are at school and George will be delighted to see you again. We'll have lunch, then you can get your things—did you leave your car at Broad Chalke? Good—Julia can drive you over to fetch it; we'll phone the stables and Goliath can stay here for the weekend—it won't be the first time . . .'

Mrs Mitchell nodding approval of her advice, sent Nicholas to fetch her husband, begged Julia to show the professor his room and tidy herself at the same time, warned them that lunch would be ready in another ten minutes or so, and went back to the kitchen.

Julia started up the stairs, she spoke over her shoulder. 'I think Mother intends you to have the guest room—Nicholas is in Jason's.' She led the way down a narrow passage at the back of the house and up two steps to a large low-ceilinged room with a low casement window. The furniture was old and beautifully polished and there was a patchwork quilt on the big bed.

'I'll get you some towels, and if there is anything else you need, Professor . . .'

'My name is Lauris.'

'Oh, is it? That's Dutch, I expect—I've not heard it before. The towels . . .' She wanted to get away although she wasn't quite sure why!

'Julia, if you don't want me to stay, tell me and I'll go. You're unhappy about Longman, aren't you— perhaps I make it worse—remind you of St Anne's . . .'

'No, no don't go. I don't mean to be . . .' She looked

up at his impassive face. 'I'm a bit muddled that's all.'

He had come to stand by her. 'Because Longman has gone to his home instead of spending the weekend with you. But he hasn't gone to the ends of the earth, Julia, only to Bristol—and you have your weekends together and holidays and once he's settled in he'll probably want to get married as soon as possible.'

Julia stared at his tie. She said on a sigh: 'You're so much nicer than I thought you were, and I've been working for you for more than three years . . .'

Which really didn't answer him at all, although strangely enough, it seemed to satisfy him.

Excepting their morning rides together with Nicholas, she saw very little of him; he took his son for long walks, spent a good deal of time with her father, and at meals, although he treated her with the utmost friendliness, he made no attempt to be alone with her. Only on Sunday as they walked back from church, planning a last ride after lunch, did he suggest casually that she might like to go back to London with him that evening. 'We'll take Nicky back on the way,' he told her, 'if you've no objection. I know that you're not on duty until one o'clock and probably intended to return on Monday morning, but the offer stands if you care to take it up.'

It seemed a good idea; it would save the tiresome business of getting herself and Wellington from Waterloo to her flat and she could use Monday morning for some shopping. She agreed at once and Nicholas, busy rubbing down Star asked, 'Couldn't you come and see us one day, Julia? When I'm home for the holidays? We could take the dogs for a walk . . .'

'A splendid idea,' observed the professor. 'Although I dare say Julia hasn't a great deal of time to spare.'

Julia didn't wait to decide if he was putting her off or encouraging her; probably neither, she didn't imagine that he was interested in her leisure hours; once or twice he had shown a surprisingly sympathetic interest in her, but she didn't set much store by that. 'Why, Nicholas, I'd like to do that—I could meet you in one of the parks. Will you write to me when you are on holiday and suggest a time and I'll see if I can arrange something.'

'Oh, super! Race you to the house, Julia.'

She allowed him to win, but only just, and then waited for the professor to catch up with them. Her cheeks were pink with the exercise then and her eyes sparkled greenly. She said a little out of breath, 'I'm getting too old for tearing round like a ten-year-old.'

The professor looked her up and down very deliberately. 'You are just the right age,' he pronounced calmly, 'and not only for tearing around.'

She was still out of breath but for a different reason now. 'I don't know what you are talking about,' she said crossly.

She saw very little of him for the rest of the day; he and her father disappeared into the study after lunch and then he and Nicholas went off for a walk before tea. Julia half expected to be asked to go with them, but she wasn't and retired to the drawing-room with her Mother and the pair of them made vague plans about her wedding. 'Although it's not much use discussing it until you have a more definite date, darling,' complained Mrs Mitchell.

Julia looked up from the game she was having with Wellington. 'No, Mother. Perhaps Nigel will know a bit more about his job and the flat when he has settled in. When do the boys break up? I'll come home for another weekend, it seems ages since I saw them. Madge is coming up for the day next week; she wants to do some shopping; I'll get a day off and see her on to the train. You don't mind having little Harry?'

'He's such a good baby. A day out will do her good. Had we better get tea I wonder? Nicholas has to be back at school by six o'clock.'

Julia got up. 'I'll get it—it'll give me something to do . . .'

She took her time setting the table, cutting sandwiches, fetching the cake and scones and jam and cream. For some reason she felt restless.

The meal was a lively one, brought to a reluctant finish by the professor's remark that if they didn't leave within the next ten minutes Nicholas would be late back.

Goodbyes said, he sent the Rolls along the narrow road; the evening was already closing in and Nicholas said happily, 'It'll soon be Christmas—do you come home, Julia?'

'No—it's a kind of unwritten law that ward sisters are on duty for at least part of Christmas Day, besides, there are the decorations and all the extra food and presents to tie up I shall be frightfully busy.'

'Oh, that's a pity—it would be nice if you could come and see us. Perhaps you'll be married by then . . .'

'Well, I don't expect to be,' said Julia slowly.

'The unexpected always happens,' observed the professor quietly, 'we have but to wait and see.'

Nicholas safely delivered at his school house, the professor took the road to London. He was silent for

a while, and Julia made no attempt to talk, perhaps
he was thinking about Nicholas; the boy had been
happy and he was devoted to his father; the two of
them must hate being apart. 'He needs a mother,'
she said out loud, voicing a thought, and almost bit
her tongue out with rage at her own foolishness. It
was a splendid chance for the professor to make one
of his biting remarks, so she was all the more
astonished when he said matter-of-factly, 'Well, he'll
have one soon.'

She had no idea why she found this statement so
unwelcome. She said brightly: 'Oh, how nice—I
didn't know . . .'

'How should you?' he wanted to know coolly, 'I
don't broadcast the details of my private life to all and
sundry.'

'I won't tell a soul,' she assured him, her voice
rather high and stiff. And fell to pondering the matter.
If it was the blonde girl she had met outside the
cinema, then he had made a bad choice; she wouldn't
do at all, neither for him or for Nicholas. She would
have to find out . . .

'It's no good guessing,' said the professor blandly,
'You'll be told in good time.'

'I'm not really interested Professor, why should I
be?'

'A moot point.' They were getting near the
motorway but at it's approach he turned off on to the
A33. 'Why aren't we going on the motorway?' Asked
Julia.

'Since I have been the cause of you cutting short
your weekend, the least I can do is take you out to
dinner.'

Julia turned her head to stare at his calm profile.

She said very coldly, 'Put like that, Professor, I have no difficulty in refusing.'

His bellow of laughter confused her. 'My dear Julia, you have called me "Professor" twice within the last few minutes. I can't think why: I've only asked you out to dinner, surely a harmless enough event. Of what are you afraid, I wonder? I suspect you don't know. You will find out in time for yourself. In the meantime, are we both to go hungry or shall we stop and eat?' He added at his most bland. 'Aren't you hungry?'

'Yes,' said Julia. Tea seemed a long while ago and a supperless evening wasn't inviting.

'Good. You are such a sensible young woman, Julia. One must admire you for that.'

He took her to Andwells Restaurant in the village of Heckfield. And very nice too, thought Julia, sitting opposite him in the pleasant room, trying to decide what to eat. She decided on Salade Niçoise, lobster Newburg and soufflé Harlequin while the professor settled for oysters, grilled steak and truffles and the cheese board.

'It is a pleasure,' said the professor silkily, 'to have a meal with someone who doesn't peck at raw carrots and toast melba.'

'I don't like carrots,' she told him pleasantly, 'probably something to do with my red hair.'

'You don't mind having such—er—striking hair?'

'Why should I? I've had it all my life and I'm used to it. When I was a little girl I used to want to be golden-haired, small and slim; I gave up wanting the impossible some years ago.'

He sat back in his chair very much at his ease. 'As I said, you are a sensible young woman, Julia.'

There was, she felt, no need to labour the point. She began on the salad, embarking at the same time on an aimless conversation about nothing much. A pity; it was such a waste of time to talk nothings with someone one could really talk to, say anything without fear of being misunderstood. She paused in mid-sentence, her fork half way to her mouth, struck by the thought that she would have no difficulty at all in saying anything which came into her head to the professor, whereas with Nigel she would need to think carefully first . . .

'You have been struck by a sudden thought,' observed her companion unerringly. 'May I know it?'

She popped some lobster into her mouth and chewed it while she thought. 'No—I don't think you'd better. It's just something . . .'

He gave her a hooded glance. 'These odd stray thoughts,' he commented vaguely. 'When do you expect to see Longman?'

She hadn't expected that. 'I don't know. He's going there this evening; he has to find out where I can stay and that sort of thing . . .'

'His parents?' murmured the professor.

She shot him a vexed look. 'I really don't know,' she told him sharply. He seemed to lose interest, for he began to talk about a number of everyday topics which took them smoothly through the rest of the meal and indeed half way to London. And after that they fell into a companionable silence until they were slowing through the outskirts.

'Have you had all your holidays for the year?' His question was so casual that she answered it promptly. 'Heavens no. We get six weeks you know; I've two more to come and several odd days owing to me.'

'Something to look forward to. You take them when you like I suppose?'

'Oh yes, although we have to fit in with whoever is to take over. Pat and I never have any trouble, she's a splendid help to me.'

'Do you travel?' He was still casual, making conversation she supposed.

'Almost never. I like to go home. Does that sound dull?'

'Not in the least; I like to go home too. By that I mean Holland . . .'

'I forget that you are Dutch. When you marry, will you live there?'

'Later on, perhaps.' He glanced sideways at her. 'My future plans are just the same as yours, Julia, undecided.'

He swung the car into her street and drew up smoothly before the house. He got out, opened her door and reached into the back for Wellington's basket, carried it into the entrance hall and stood looking down at her. 'Well, I'll say good night, Julia. On Tuesday it will be "Good morning, Sister Mitchell".'

'Like being two people,' said Julia. 'It's a pity . . .' She stopped and then went on, 'Thank you for the lift. It was a nice weekend.'

'Delightful. We hardly had a cross word.'

He was staring at her and she studied his face carefully, suddenly wishful of learning every line of it. Not so young, perhaps, but still good looks to be reckoned with—indeed, he would never lose them, however old he was. When he wasn't being peppery he was one of the nicest people she had ever known. That didn't include Nigel, of course, she added hastily to herself, she mustn't forget Nigel.'

She said hesitantly, 'Would you like a cup of coffee?' and then blushed when he refused. She had been silly to ask him; she was already Sister Mitchell again and he was Professor van der Wagema, who would doubtless be in a filthy temper on Tuesday and whose mind must be entirely taken up with thoughts of his future wife. Suddenly she wished with all her heart that he was Lauris again and not the professor. Her thoughts, sadly muddled, became chaotic, Nigel dwindled into a tiny cardboard figure in another world and the professor loomed larger than life. It wouldn't do at all. She said urgently: 'Oh, dear whatever shall I do?' and snatched up Wellington in his basket and flew upstairs without another word.

The professor watched her go, smiling to himself.

CHAPTER SIX

IN her flat, Julia let an impatient Wellington out of his basket, gave him his supper and put the kettle on; a cup of tea might soothe her back to normal. But it needed more than that; how did one smother a sudden fierce onrush of feelings with tea? And had she gone stark raving mad? Wasn't she engaged to Nigel and hadn't she been in love with him for at least two years?

She let her tea grow cold while she sat down to think it out. Perhaps she had been in love with him to begin with; she was still fond of him but all the glamour and excitement had gone a long time ago, only she had never admitted it. And now Professor van der Wagema had taken over; she had been in love with him for quite a time, she realised now, but hadn't known it and the awful thing was that he regarded her as he always had done, a ward sister who carried out his wishes meticulously and who argued with him when she saw fit to do so. His recent friendliness she put down to his forthcoming marriage; love must have softened him.

She drank tepid tea; it was a situation she would have to face up to. The professor must never find out, for a start, but he wasn't likely to; when he wasn't totally absorbed in his work, he would be totally absorbed in his wife, and Nicholas, of course. She hoped fleetingly that the boy would be happy; he had had his father to himself for a long time. And how about Nigel—she would have to talk to him, explain, if she could, make him understand although she shrank from telling him the truth, at least a good part of it. She was fond of him and it would hurt his pride needlessly if she told him that she had fallen in love with someone else. That was something she would have to keep to herself.

She got ready for bed and then lay in the dark with Wellington curled up against her. She had been buoyed up with high-minded resolutions, but now all she felt was misery. It was unthinkable to marry Nigel now; a future with no purpose was just as unthinkable but it was something she would have to get used to. She would start at once by closing her eyes and going to sleep.

She slept but she awakened early, and since lying in bed and thinking was of no use, she got up, had an early breakfast, tidied her room, attended to Wellington's wants, went shopping and then walked the long way round to the hospital. She started up the stairs, going slowly, reluctant to start the day. At least, she told herself, the professor had no round until the next day which would give her time to pull herself together.

He was there, at the top to the staircase and she paled a little when she saw him. His genial, 'Well, well, Sister Mitchell, I must applaud your zeal; last time we met you were almost, but not quite, late,' did nothing to improve the situation.

She looked at him so wildly that he said in a quite different voice. 'Are you ill, Julia?' and took a step towards her, but she flew past him without answering, only to find him right by her, holding the ward doors open, an arm on hers, leading her willy-nilly to her office.

He pushed her gently into her chair and closed the

door and then stood in front of it, his great arms folded against his massive chest.

'Well?' he asked.

She studied the desk before her; the night nurses report book, the off duty, the pile of forms ready for her to make out and sign. She would have to answer him, he wasn't a man to be fobbed off with fairy tales. She took a breath: 'I'm quite well, thank you, Professor. I'm a little tired, that's all.' She kept her eyes on his waistcoat and her voice steady.

'Lying awake thinking about Longman?' His voice was dry.

She nodded. 'Yes. I can't—that is, I don't think it would work out—him and me getting married. And I'd rather not talk about it.'

'Balderdash,' declared the professor and left the door to sit on a corner of her desk. 'Let's have it, otherwise you're going to muddle through the day and get into a fine pickle. Does he know?'

'Of course not—I only made up my mind during the night.'

'Then you'll have to tell him, won't you? When do you have your next day off?'

'At the end of the week. That's a silly question just when I'm trying to explain . . .'

'Not at all silly, when you know me better you will find out that I don't ask silly questions. I have to go to Bristol on Friday, you can come with me and see him. Perhaps you can work out something between you—it may not be as bad as you think.'

She said stubbornly, 'I shan't change my mind.'

'A woman's privilege, at least give him a chance. Things are always worse at night.'

She glanced at him briefly; he looked kind and

encouraging and he really wanted to put things right. The irony of it struck her so forcibly that she wanted to laugh. Instead she said soberly, 'Thank you, it's kind of you to want to help. I'll come with you if I may and talk to Nigel.'

He was looking austere again; perhaps he was already regretting his offer. 'That's if you really are going?' she added uncertainly.

'I'm going. We'll have to leave early—eight o'clock? I'll be at the front entrance.' He got off the desk, and turned on his heel and went out of the office.

She got through the day. It was a good thing that they were busy, with patients being discharged and others being admitted and a more than usual number going to X-Ray and Physiotherapy, not to mention the few trouble makers complaining bitterly about anything and everything they could dream up, and hindering the nurses from getting on with the routine chores around the ward. She went off duty in the evening and hurried back to a welcoming Wellington and the prospect of a solitary evening. There was always the chance that Nigel would 'phone, of course, although she didn't expect him too. All the same, she cooked her supper with one ear listening for Mrs Humbert, who lived on the ground floor, nearest the 'phone box, to bellow up the stairs to her. But nothing happened; she washed her stockings and her hair and went early to bed.

The professor came to do his round exactly on time, presenting a calm, austere front to those around him. His 'Good morning, Sister Mitchell' was uttered in brisk, impersonal accents so that she found herself wondering which was the real man, this impersonal, polite rather learned man, or Lauris, the satisfying companion she had grown to love.

But if he could be brisk so could she. The round was conducted in an atmosphere of efficient and unhurried calm and the subsequent coffee drinking done to the accompaniment of small talk. She saw him go with relief even while she longed for him so much to stay. He was exactly the same when he did his second round on Thursday, and he made no mention of the following morning's journey. She found it difficult to remain cool and calm for the rest of the day, which seemed twice as long as usual, but finally she went off duty, arranged with Mrs Humbert to feed Wellington while she was away the next day, put everything ready for the morning, and did the ironing, watching the television with one eye and trying not to think. There had been no word from Nigel and she wasn't sure if that was a good thing or not, but even if he wrote or 'phoned she wasn't going to change her mind.

It was a chilly morning, she fed Wellington, handed the key to Mrs Humbert, and wearing the new tweed suit she had bought on her last shopping expedition to Regent Street, walked quickly to the hospital, wondering as she went why the professor hadn't offered to pick her up from her flat.

The Rolls was there and he was at the wheel. He got out when he saw her coming, and opened her door with a quiet good morning and got back in beside her.

'If you're wondering why I didn't come to fetch you I had to see a patient in the private wing before he goes home today. Did you have breakfast?'

'Yes—no, that is, a cup of tea and a biscuit.'

'We'll stop on the way. There's a place at Sonning, we can turn off just before Reading and get back on to the M4 easily enough.' He added: 'You'll fight better on a full stomach.'

'I have no intention of fighting,' said Julia haughtily.

'You're a little fool if you don't—it's your future, isn't it worth fighting for?'

Unanswerable without giving herself away. She mumbled something and looked out of the window.

'That's a pretty outfit—very fetching, but then it's an occasion, isn't it?'

'You're doing it deliberately, aren't you? Needling me?'

'Yes, otherwise you'll lapse into apathy and make no attempt to solve your problems.'

'Supposing I can't see him?'

'My dear girl, even the busiest of surgeons has to stop for a bite to eat, there's no reason why you shouldn't enjoy a snack with him. After all it doesn't take long to clear the air one way or the other.'

She sat silent then, rehearsing what she was going to say, distracted from a variety of suitable speeches by his calm, solid bulk beside her. She couldn't turn to look at him, of course, but she could watch his large, well kept hands on the wheel; far more satisfying than trying to think what to say to Nigel. She felt mean about Nigel, although she had a sneaking feeling that when he got over the shock he might be relieved. He would be able to forge ahead with his career without having to worry about supporting a wife and children. And his parents would be pleased, she was sure of that. She looked away and really tried to compose a soothing speech which wouldn't hurt Nigel's feelings. It was a relief when the professor swept the Rolls off the motorway and presently stopped before the White Hart where they ate a splendid breakfast before driving on again.

They were threading their way through Bristol's busy streets by half past ten and a few minutes later the professor parked the Rolls in the hospital's courtyard. For a moment he sat quiet, then he undid his seat belt, stretched out a hand and did the same for her: 'Well,' he said, 'here we are.'

'Yes. Thank you—it was a lovely drive. Should I go to the porter's lodge, do you think?'

'You'll come with me.'

He got out of the car and went round to her door and gave her a hand. It felt cool and firm and reassuring; it would have been nice if she could have hung on to it; it might stop her confidence from oozing out of the soles of her best shoes. They walked side by side through the massive door and across an imposing stretch of marbled floor to the porter's lodge.

She couldn't hear what the professor was saying for his back took up the whole of the little opening through which one addressed the porter inside, but presently he turned to face her. 'You're lucky; Longman isn't operating until two o'clock. He's doing a round at the moment but will be free in about an hour. We'll have coffee.'

He took her arm and hurried her outside again while she protested: 'But what about you? You had an appointment . . .'

'Midday—a working lunch.'

'Oh—but how do you know about Nigel? Did you speak to him on the 'phone?'

'No, the porter has the theatre timetable in his Lodge and the ward sister of the Surgical Ward where he is at present, rang down to say that he was there. All I did was to leave a message asking him to come to the visitors' waiting room when he was free. I am assured by the porter that we can reckon on an hour before he will finish.'

'But oughtn't I just to wait here? Supposing he's early and I'm not back?'

She was being walked inexorably out of the courtyard and into the street beyond. 'There's a coffee shop close by.' The professor sounded positively soothing.

She drank her coffee obediently, listening to the professor's casual conversation, knowing that he didn't expect her to take much part in it. Despite herself, her eyes flew to the clock every few minutes and when he suggested that she should go and do something to her face, she almost leapt from her chair. 'Do I look awful?'

He studied her gravely.' No, you look very pretty, but a little pale. You'll do very well.'

Thus encouraged, she peered in the enormous mirror in the powder room and decided that however awful she felt inside, she looked much as usual. And Lauris had called her very pretty. She savoured that for a moment before reminding herself that he was being kind, nothing more.

The waiting room was totally neutral; off white walls with very modern prints, steel chairs with canvas seats, a conventional round table in the centre, its glass top neatly patterned with last year's magazines, green-patterned curtains at the windows. Why, wondered Julia, sitting uneasily, did hospital authorities go nap on green?

She had insisted on going back to the hospital at least ten minutes too soon and the professor hadn't argued with her, but wordlessly escorted her the short distance from the coffee shop, ushered her in to the waiting room, told her briefly that he would be in the Rolls at two o'clock, and gone away.

'He might have given me just one word of encouragement,' said Julia to the empty room. The one consolation was that if he had said two o'clock, he had meant it. Her mind was empty; all the careful speeches she had been rehearsing had melted into thin air, but somehow that didn't matter any more; words would come when she saw Nigel.

He came ten minutes later, stopping on the threshold in utter astonishment.

'My dear Julia, the last person I expected to see.' He crossed the room to where she stood. 'Have you come after that job? I heard it was being advertised, though I should warn you that there are at least two of the junior sisters who are after it; it would be better if you waited until those two posts come vacant next summer . . .'

He kissed her. 'Well, what's the matter? Did you come by train?' He frowned slightly. 'I can't think why you came—I did say I'd write.'

'So you did, you said you'd 'phone too,' she reminded him gently. 'I dare say you've been very busy.'

'Oh I have—you've no idea; I can see that I'm not going to have much time to myself, but it's a splendid job and it'll lead to other things, too.' He gave her a thoughtful look. 'It may be better if we don't marry in too much of a hurry, Julia; I'll have to put my back into the work here and it'll take up all my time . . .'

She took a deep breath. 'Nigel, I've been thinking all this week. I believe that we should call the whole thing off—us, I mean, getting married. Perhaps if I

were ten years younger, I'd wait, but I'm thirty and I
need to decide my future too, you know. I think—I'm
sure—I want to stick to my career; there are several
good jobs I could go after. If you were willing to
marry now perhaps I'd change my mind, but it would
be a great hindrance to you—to your career. So may
we part the best of friends and no hard feelings?'

He said sharply, 'You're throwing me over? Just like
that? I had no idea that you were so ambitious. I
thought you loved me . . .'

'I'm very fond of you, Nigel, and I did love you,
truly I do think I did, only we've gone on too long,
haven't we? If you'll be honest, you'll admit that.' She
achieved a smile of sorts. 'Carve yourself a career for a
couple of years and then find a nice girl—a nice young
girl.' She added quietly: 'I'm right, aren't I?'

'You mean it's better for both of us——' He
sounded relieved to have been given a loophole.
'Funny you should say that—Mother said the same
thing when I was home. You think it's the right thing
to do?'

She nodded, fighting the tears. Surely he could have
shown a little regret? Hadn't he loved her either? Or
had he, like her, lost that love during the last year? She
should be thankful, she mused, that he was taking it so
well; it would have been nice if she could have told
him about the professor but the idea was absurd; it
was a secret she would have to keep to herself for ever.

She took the ring off her finger and held it out.
'You'll always be a friend,' she told him, 'we had nice
times together, didn't we? But better to part now than
marry and regret it afterwards. You'll get to the top,
Nigel, and you'll get there much faster without me.'

He took the ring and put it in a pocket. He said

without conceit, 'Yes, I shall. What do your people say?'

'I've not told them, but I will. Say all the right things to your mother and father, won't you? And when you come to London look me up. When you are an eminent consultant and I'm running a hospital, we'll meet and talk over old times.'

The relief on his face convinced her that he wasn't going to be permanently hurt. She gave him her hand and lifted her face for his kiss.

'All the best, Nigel, dear; when you feel like it, write to me.'

He kissed her quite heartily. 'Of course. You're going back now, I suppose? Sorry I haven't the time to take you out to lunch.'

They walked to the door together and she wished him another cheerful goodbye as she went past him. He hadn't wanted to know how she had come or how she would go and there was no point in telling him. She walked without haste down the corridor and at the end turned to wave to him but he had already disappeared.

She went out of the hospital and started to walk along the street. She didn't much care where she was going; it wasn't yet half-past twelve and they weren't leaving before two o'clock, she had time to kill. She went down Rupert Street and into Colston Street and round into Park Row past the University and fetched up at length in Tyndall's Park where she sat down, shivering a little, for it had grown chilly.

Well, she had done what she intended to do and thankfully, without doing more than temporarily bruising Nigel's feelings. She suspected that so great was his interest in his work, that he would have little time to regret their parting. And she had to admit to herself that she was glad that she had done it now, at least she'd been honest with herself without doing any harm to anyone, the future was another matter but she wasn't going to think about that. She sat, her mind empty, until she saw that it was time for her to go back. She had to hurry, for she hadn't left herself much time; the professor was in the car, sitting impassively as though he had all the time in the world and she muttered excuses as he opened the door and she got in.

He didn't say a word but started the car and drove smoothly through the streets and on to the motorway. He sent the Rolls down the fast lane before he said, 'You've had no lunch. We'll stop at a service station.'

'I'm not hungry, thank you.' Julia's voice was small.

'Then we'll have a pot of tea.'

The service station was a few miles ahead of them; he turned into it and they got out and entered its warm stuffiness, redolent of chips and more faintly, fried onions. The place was crowded and he took her arm and steered her between the tables before he found two seats at a table for four; the other two seats were occupied by an elderly man with a straggly moustache and a pale wisp of a woman in a deplorable hat. 'Stay there,' counselled the professor and made his way to the counter.

He came back presently with a tray of tea and a plate of buttered tea cakes, set everything neatly on the table, and sat down opposite to her. The tea he poured was richly brown and he sugared it lavishly. 'Drink that,' he told her gently, and put a tea cake on the plate and put it in front of her.

She ate and drank meekly, listening with half an ear

to the conversation he was enjoying with their companions. Yes, they were on their way to London, he agreed in answer to the man's question, and yes, he agreed again, the motorway was a blessing.

'Bin ter see the daughter,' said the man, ' 'ad a baby last week, she did. Nice little feller. You got kids?' His eyes slid to Julia.

'I have a son,' said the professor calmly.

'Nuthin like it,' observed the man. 'Kids—make life worthwhile, they do. Don't they, Em?'

His wife nodded. 'We've 'ad six, good children, the lot of 'em.' She turned bright friendly eyes on Julia, 'You'll be looking forward to adding to the family, I've no doubt.'

Julia went slowly pink; her smile was shy and it was the professor who answered. 'Oh, we are—I only hope they'll give us the pleasure your family have given you.'

'That's right. Well, we'll be on our way—got ter get ter Barking and the old car don't run all that well these days.' He beamed at them both. 'So long—bin nice meeting yer.'

'Ta-ta,' said his wife cheerfully and the professor, not to be outdone, replied 'Ta-ta,' and then poured the second cup.

'Two happy people,' he commented. 'Feeling better?'

'Yes, thank you. I'm quite—I'm quite all right, I enjoyed the tea. What time shall we be in London?'

He glanced at his watch. 'A couple of hours—just in nice time to hit the rush hour.'

'Oh, we shouldn't have stopped—if you want to go out this evening . . .'

'I'm not in any hurry. Shall we go?'

The afternoon was sliding into early dusk and the road stretched ahead, car lights weaving to and fro, intent on getting somewhere fast. Julia closed her eyes, assailed by a mixture of feelings; to be sitting beside the man she loved was bliss, it more than outweighed the uncertainty of the future, but the bliss wasn't going to last long, tomorrow she would be back on the ward and on Tuesday morning Lauris would do his round and she would be Sister Mitchell, someone he had helped over a sticky few days. And he was so nice, she thought sleepily; he had stood up when the two people at their table had left; she had seen the delight at that small, seldom seen courtesy on the woman's face. He could be thoroughly unpleasant too . . . she slept.

She didn't wake until he stopped the car outside her flat. It took her a moment to realise where she was. 'Oh, Lord—I'm sorry I went to sleep.' She began to scramble upright, embarking on a muddled speech of thanks as she did so.

'Not so fast,' said the professor calmly. 'I'm coming in with you.'

The flat struck chill as she opened the door although Wellington's welcome was warm. Julia went to light the gas fire and switch on a couple of table lamps and since the professor had come right into the room with her and was pulling the curtains and filling the kettle she perforce asked him if he would like coffee.

'I'll see to it—you get Wellington's supper. Is there anything to eat?'

'Bacon and eggs and some things for salad in the fridge.'

'Good, I'll stay to supper if you'll ask me?'

Julia was scooping out cat food from a tin but she paused to look at him. 'But don't you want to go home? I mean go out or something?'

'No, it's Martha's evening out and I have no plans.'

'Oh, I just thought . . .' She caught the gleam in his eye. 'Would eggs and bacon do?' she added, 'And a salad, or would you rather have scrambled eggs?'

'Bacon and eggs will do nicely. Shall we have coffee first? Is there anything to drink?'

'Beer—I keep a few bottles for—for Nigel.' She bent over Wellington's saucer. 'And there's some sherry in that cupboard. I haven't any whisky or gin.'

'Beer will be splendid.' He made the coffee and put the tray on a small table before the fire. 'Now tell me; you'll feel much better when you've said everything out loud. Otherwise your thoughts just mill around inside your head, getting worse by the minute.'

She sipped her coffee. 'I don't know where to begin . . . I had to wait a little while and—and Nigel amazed me he was so very surprised to see me—he thought I'd gone after a job and told me to wait until next year . . . He suggested that we put off getting married for the time being because he wanted to concentrate on his job. So I said I thought we oughtn't to marry at all and he was quite relieved.' She sniffed and blew her beautiful nose, stubbornly refusing to cry. 'We're still friends.'

'And what do you intend to do now, Julia?'

She gave him a cross look. 'I'm sure I don't know— I haven't had time to think about it.'

He said decisively, 'Then stay where you are for the moment until you can think straight.' He refilled their coffee cups. 'Will you promise me that, Julia?'

'Why?'

He said patiently: 'Because one often acts unwisely in the heat of the moment. Give yourself time, dear girl, so promise?'

'Very well, but I'll have to do something, I don't think I can go on at St Anne's.'

His ready agreement left her feeling disappointed, but he left her no time to brood.

'I'll make the salad if you see to the bacon and eggs,' he offered.

Over their supper he talked about Nicholas. 'It's an occasional holiday the weekend after next, I must make arrangements to be free.'

'Oh, I'd forgotten the boys will be home too—I'm glad it's my weekend off . . .' She stopped and went pink, for it sounded as though she were fishing for a lift, but apparently he hadn't given it a thought.

'It will be Christmas before we can turn round. We shall spend it here of course, but go to Holland for New Year—we always do. A family gathering of quite formidable proportions.'

He helped her wash up before he went, not mentioning Nigel again, but talking about the ward and his patients, keeping to the lighter side of their work and finally taking a casual leave of her. 'I'll not be in again until the round on Tuesday.' He told her at the door, 'Dick's on until Monday anyway, and it's not take in, is it?'

The room seemed very empty after he had gone.

It had been a long day and she was tired, she went to sleep at once to wake very early and lie and worry. She was unhappy about Nigel; she might not love him anymore, but they had been close for more than two years and he was going to leave a gap in her life. She was almost sure that he would recover far more quickly than she; he had a new and absorbing job and different surroundings whereas she was going to be constantly reminded of him while she was at St Anne's. All the same she had done the right thing, she was sure of that. It was the professor who worried her most of all; it would have been so much easier if he hadn't become so friendly and easy to talk to. True, he had his starchy moments, but even those she no longer minded; how could she when she loved him so very much? But she didn't think that she could stay at St Anne's, hoping each day that she would see him and knowing that to him she was the Women's Medical ward sister who had hit a bad patch and to whom he had given a helping hand.

She got dressed and had her breakfast with Wellington beside her. She would go home on her next weekend off and talk to her mother and take her advice.

The ward was full, with several seriously ill patients; Julia was too busy to think about her own problems and since she went to midday dinner late there wasn't much time for gossip. All the same, since several of her closer friends were there she took the bull by the horns and told them that she and Nigel had decided to break off their engagement.

'We wouldn't be able to marry for at least two years and I know that Nigel wanted to be free to get on with his work and get ahead.' She added as cheerfully as she could, 'He's bound to be successful.'

They were all nice about it, not saying much, suggesting that she spent the evening with them at the cinema. She didn't really want to and said feebly, 'There's Wellington . . .'

'Go to the flat and feed him and pick us up here; we can have coffee and a sandwich before the film . . .'

Which passed the evening very well, and tomorrow, she reminded herself, Lauris would be doing his round and she would see him again.

He wasn't in a good mood; his greeting was so austere; he looked at her with a detached air, just as though he couldn't quite remember who she was so that vexation began to bubble inside her. She answered his questions about the patients with cold exactitude and presently, over coffee and biscuits, discussed the weather at length and with a lack of originality which caused Dick to look at her in some astonishment. In all the time he had known her, she had never bored him as she was now doing. He glanced at the professor and saw that something was amusing him very much although Julia had said nothing which was even faintly worthy of a smile. There was a distinct atmosphere too; at any moment, taking into account Julia's fiery hair, the pair of them would be crossing swords. He put down his coffee cup and mentioned the severe haemoptesis in Men's Medical and the professor got to his feet, bade Julia an icily polite good morning and left the ward.

She didn't see him again that week. Dick did the Friday round, telling her that the professor had already left for his weekend. 'Spending it with his son, he tells me. You've met him, haven't you?'

They talked in a desultory fashion over their coffee and as he got up to go he asked: 'Isn't it your weekend off, Julia? Will Pat be here?'

Julia nodded. 'Yes, there's nothing very worrying now is there? And she's capable of coping with anything that might turn up.'

She went home that evening, to be met by her father and driven through the chilly autumn dusk. 'How are the boys?' she wanted to know.

'Splendid. They got home this morning before lunch and they haven't stopped eating. They're doing pretty well this term, work wise, although rugger seems to be the main interest.'

'Nice,' said Julia and was thankful that he hadn't asked about Nigel.

The boys rushed to meet her, both talking at once and once Wellington was out of his basket and sitting with Gyp by the Aga and she had hugged her mother and gone up to her room to tidy herself for supper, she felt as though she had been home for ever.

As she reached the last stair Jason came into the hall. 'There's a surprise for you in the drawing room,' he told her.

'Not another dog? Gyp would never stand that?' He shook his head, grinning at her. 'Not Granny?' Granny lived miles away in Essex and seldom travelled. 'The vicar?' she hissed in a whisper as he opened the door.

Her father was there, so were Gregory, Nicholas and the professor gathered round the long table at one end of the big room.

'There you are, my dear,' declared her father, 'we're just setting things up for a game of Scrabble after supper—you'll play, of course.'

Nicholas had started towards her. 'Julia, isn't this fun? We're staying here for the weekend, Mr Mitchell suggested it—can we go riding? Gregory says you will . . .'

'Why not? How nice to see you again.' She gave him a warm smile, 'And what a surprise.' They walked to the table and she said with commendable calm: 'Hullo, Lauris.'

He came and took her hand. 'How we do keep

meeting?' he said lightly. 'I do hope you weren't counting on a quiet weekend!'

'Not with the boys at home. Don't tell me you play Scrabble too?'

'I'm good at it,' he told her smugly.

They had supper then, a boisterous meal, and it wasn't until its end that Mrs Mitchell asked during a pause in the talk: 'Have you heard from Nigel, Julia? Does he like his job? You'll be going to Bristol for a weekend? Perhaps he'll change his mind about getting married . . .?'

Julia looked at her, her green eyes stricken but before she could speak the professor asked smoothly: 'Have you been to Bristol lately, Mrs Mitchell? It is more changed than other cities—around the docks especially. I was there recently . . .' He went on talking and Mrs Mitchell, aware that something was wrong, allowed herself to be swept into a lengthy discussion about the modernising of towns.

They left the table presently everyone helping to clear away the dishes and when Mrs Mitchell would have sent them all out of the kitchen, the men declared that they would wash up while the boys made the coffee. It was a good chance to get her mother alone and Julia took it. She urged her into her father's study and shut the door. 'Mother, I didn't have a chance to tell you before—Nigel and I have broken off our engagement—Lauris was going to Bristol last week and he gave me a lift and I spent an hour with Nigel— you see, I hadn't heard from him and then when I did see him he wanted to put the wedding off even longer and I knew it wouldn't work.'

Mrs Mitchell studied her daughter's face. 'Yes, darling. You don't love each other any more?'

'No, Mother.'

'Then that's all for the best, darling. I'm sorry because you are unhappy, but in a way I'm glad too. I'll tell your father, presently and the boys if they ask. They never liked Nigel very much—he doesn't play rugger.' She added apologetically: 'Of course, that's a silly reason, isn't it? That's why they are all over Lauris; he played for his hospital . . .'

Julia opened her eyes. 'Did he, now? Mother how did he get here for the weekend?'

Her mother said innocently, 'By car, dear.'

'Yes, Mother, but did you invite him or did he just turn up?'

Mrs Mitchell looked shocked. 'Oh, he wouldn't do that. Your father 'phoned to see if Nicholas could spend the weekend with the boys and Lauris said that he had planned to come down and spend a day or two with Nicky, so your father suggested that he should come here too. I mean, that's sensible, isn't it, dear?'

Julia agreed and wondered silently what the professor's fiancée thought about it.

It was impossible to be unhappy in such cheerful company; she was up early helping her mother to get breakfast and then, the household chores done she joined the three boys for a walk over the hills and after lunch they were all driven over to the stables and rode back with Jason leading the professor's horse while he drove the car. Nicholas, being the youngest, had Star. They lost no time in getting in a ride before the early dusk. Coming home, seeing the lighted old house from the lane, Julia thought how pleasant life could be, even when things weren't going just as one would like.

They all went to church in the morning and then rode again after one of Mrs Mitchell's splendid

Sunday dinners. The afternoon ended too soon, the boys and the professor took the horses back and Mr Mitchell drove over to bring them home again and she and Nicholas saw to Star and made much of Jane. And presently, very pretty in her tweed suit, Julia carried in the tea. They ate it round the fire in the drawing-room, crumpets, and sandwiches and a cake to cut at and endless cups to drink. The boys weren't going back until the next day and she had heard the professor agreeing to take the boys into Salisbury in the morning, so he would be staying too, although she wasn't sure of that. She hadn't been alone with him for long enough to ask and she reminded herself severely that it was no concern of hers, anyway, whether he stayed or went.

She had planned to catch an evening train and with an anxious eye on the clock she reminded her father quietly that it was time for him to drive her into Salisbury.

Mr Mitchell, deep in a discussion on Greek mythology looked vague. 'Eh? What, my dear? Didn't I tell you? Lauris has offered to drive you . . .'

'I have to run up to town,' Lauris' voice was blandly casual. 'I'll be glad to give you a lift if I may?' He stood up, 'And before we go, I've a suggestion to make. Jason and Gregory are coming over to Holland with us at the end of term—Nicky always pays a visit for a few days before Christmas—why don't you come too? I can't possibly cope with three boys on my own.'

She was so startled that she could think of nothing to say and he said easily, 'No need to say yes or no now, but I think you would enjoy it.'

The boys took up the chorus, all talking at once. Of course she must go with them, declared Jason, it was the chance of a life time and what had she intended to do with her week's holiday, anyway? He stopped and went red, because his mother had told him before tea about the broken engagement and probably Julia had been going to spend her leave with Nigel. Well, all the more reason why she should go away with them; she'd have no time to mope. He renewed his wheedlings with the two boys and Julia, recovering from her surprise, burst out laughing. 'Look, give me a little while to get used to the idea,' she begged. 'You meant it?' she addressed herself to the professor. 'I mean, it's not a joke?'

'I meant it—can you think of any reason why you shouldn't join us?'

'Yes, I can. One very good one.'

He smiled. 'She won't mind,' he said softly. 'I won't bother you for an answer until I see you next week. Is that a bargain?'

She nodded. But she asked urgently as she kissed her mother goodbye, 'Mother, do you think it's a good idea?'

'Yes, love, it's just what you need. Come home again as soon as you can. It was a pity that Madge couldn't come today. Never mind, she'll come next time.'

Julia got into the Rolls, the boys swarming round, shouting cheerfully and waving their arms.

'Anyone would think we were going to the other side of the world,' said Julia.

'A delightful prospect, but at the moment, not feasible,' replied the professor.

CHAPTER SEVEN

NEITHER Julia nor the professor had much to say as he sent the Rolls tearing towards London, but their silence was a friendly one and Julia sat drowsily, uncaring of the future for the moment, it was enough to be sitting beside Lauris even though the next time they met he would look down his nose at her and address her as 'Sister'. They were within a few miles of London when he said quietly: 'I hope you will give me the pleasure of dining with me, Julia.'

She was so taken aback that she stammered. 'Oh—well, it's very kind of you but what about Wellington?'

'He's asleep, he had a good meal before we left and will be hours sleeping it off. Besides, we shan't be all that time; I have to be back at Mrs Mitchell's some time tonight—the key is under the large stone on the left of the door.' And when she didn't answer, 'We'll go to a grill room. You don't feel like cooking, do you?'

Indeed she didn't and she said so. 'That settles it then,' he said firmly. They were already approaching the West End, presently he turned into Carlos Place and stopped outside the Connaught Hotel.

'Not here,' said Julia quite sharply, 'I'm not dressed for it.'

'The grill room,' explained the professor placidly, 'there's nothing wrong with your clothes.' He ushered her out and they went through the imposing entrance and were given a table for two in a quiet corner.

'You look uneasy,' he commented, settling himself opposite to her.

'It's not my business,' began Julia, aware that she was just asking for one of his nasty remarks but none the less compelled to speak. 'But I don't think I should be here, having dinner with you when you are getting married to someone else?'

'Why not? She is a sensible girl, and I think—I know that she trusts me. We are, after all, colleagues at work, not secret lovers.'

Julia, with a heightened colour, met his eyes squarely. 'Does she know about me, then?'

'Of course,'

'Well, as long as she wouldn't mind.' Her green eyes searched his impassive face. 'But don't you want to be with her?'

'Indeed I do. She's been away for the weekend.'

There seemed nothing more to be said on the matter, indeed, she had the sneaking feeling that she had been making too much of it altogether; she accepted the menu offered her, agreed that sherry would be very nice and applied herself to choosing her dinner. She chose smoked salmon with brown bread and butter, an omelette Diplomate because it had truffles in it, and she had never eaten any, and at her companion's suggestion, peaches poached in champagne, a delicious meal which somehow made life seem quite possible again. They didn't sit long over their coffee and when Julia voiced doubts about Wellington's displeasure if he found himself incarcerated for much longer, the professor called for the bill and they went back to the car.

The streets were fairly empty now and the drive took only a very short time. In the shabby little street, outside her own door, she thanked him nicely for the ride and her dinner, but all the same, he still got out of the car, took Wellington's basket and her overnight bag and went up the stairs to her own front door. But he didn't stay, he set Wellington down on the floor, put her bag carefully on a chair, and said cheerfully: 'Well, I'll be off. See you during the week. Good night, Julia.'

And he had gone, her hasty good night wasted on the empty air.

Curled up in bed presently, with the kitten tucked under one arm, it struck her that he had said nothing more about going to Holland with the boys. Had he really meant it, she wondered and he might have had something more to say about it if he really had. She hadn't agreed either and she wasn't going to, she told herself firmly, unless he renewed his invitation. And even then, she told herself sleepily, I may not go, aware that she had every intention of going.

She had too much to do on Monday to worry about it and there was a letter for her from Nigel which she forbore to open until she was back in her flat that evening. She opened it reluctantly, half afraid that he had thought better of their parting and wanted to try again. But she need not have worried on that score; it was a nice letter, even if a shade pompous, wishing her all the best for the future, allowing that they had made a wise decision even if a painful one and enlarging on the splendid opportunities he hoped for.

She read it carefully, relieved that he was already recovering, thinking ruefully that he was far more concerned about his own future than hers.

She tore the letter up, put the pieces tidily in the waste paper basket and made herself a pot of tea. She wasn't a conceited woman, but it was a little depressing to be dismissed so easily after more than two years.

She drank her tea and forced herself to consider her future. She didn't really want to leave St Anne's but since she had the choice, it would be sensible to leave; it would be like tearing her heart out not to see Lauris again, but meeting him on their old footing once he was married was rather more than she could manage. She would try and stay in London and she had as good a chance as anyone if she applied for a post in one of the other teaching hospitals if and when one became vacant. She might have to wait a little while but that didn't matter so much once she had made up her mind. She must be sensible she reminded herself.

It was hard to be sensible the next morning as she went down the ward to meet him when he came to do his round. There seemed to be more people than usual with him; students and the woman social worker who had brought along an assistant for some reason or other. And old Doctor Knowles who had retired years ago, when Julia was still a junior nurse and who came very occasionally to go round his old wards as a guest. She wished everyone good morning and blushed when the old man observed, 'Julia Mitchell—prettier than ever I do declare. Why aren't you married with a clutch of babies? Didn't I hear that you were going to marry young Longman?'

She hated herself for blushing but answered composedly enough. 'We've decided not to marry after all, sir.'

'H'm, well, better now than later, I suppose, but a great waste.' He beamed at her. 'Professor van der

Wagema most kindly invited me to go round with him. Some interesting cases I believe . . .'

The round went smoothly, if rather more slowly than usual. Doctor Knowles might be old, but he hadn't lost his skill and the professor deferred very nicely to him on several points of diagnosis. As they walked away from the last bed, he rubbed his hands together and enquired hopefully, 'Coffee?'

Julia ushered him into the office and sat him down at the desk; it left very little room by the time Dick and the professor had settled themselves on the radiators and she had perched on the stool the professor had fetched from the landing outside. It was over the coffee that Doctor Knowles wanted to know what had happened to Mrs Collins. 'A most interesting case,' he commented, 'and a remarkable recovery. Where is she now?'

'At my house,' said the professor. 'My housekeeper wanted someone to mend and polish the silver and so on, and Mrs Collins seemed just right for the job.'

'You've always been a man to help lame dogs over stiles,' declared Doctor Knowles and ignored his colleague's frown. 'How's that boy of yours?'

'Doing very well and making friends at school. Julia's father is coaching him and he and her brothers have struck up the beginnings of a friendship. They are all going over to Holland for a few days as soon as the holidays start.'

He turned his dark gaze on Julia and added blandly, 'Julia has been invited to go with them.'

'Splendid, splendid,' boomed Doctor Knowles happily. 'A little light relief from this job, eh, my dear?'

Julia gave the professor a look which would have

shaken a lesser man. 'I haven't yet decided,' she said coldly.

'You're free tomorrow?' asked the professor, smiling charmingly at her. 'I hope you will spare the time to discuss things with me.' He added in the tone of a kindly uncle. 'I'll collect you about eleven o'clock, if that suits you?' His avuncular manner became even more pronounced. 'We can iron out any small difficulties.'

Dick and Doctor Knowles were looking at her and smiling; she said with a touch of peevishness, 'Very well, Professor, I'm not doing anything in the morning.'

She wasn't doing anything in the afternoon either but she would think up something; a lunch date with an old friend; a mythical aunt expecting a visit . . .

She saw them off the ward presently, very dignified, and careful to avoid the professor's eye.

It was cold and grey when she got up the next morning, she looked after Wellington, cooked the breakfast, and dressed herself warmly in a jersey dress and the well-cut wool coat she had saved for; she liked good clothes even though her wardrobe was small and now she got into her new boots with the smug feeling that she was looking her best. It was too cold to forego wearing a hat; she pulled a velvet beret on top of her bright hair, took a last look at her person in the spotty mirror behind the wardrobe door, gave Wellington a hug, picked up her bag and gloves, and prepared to go. It was five minutes over the hour and when she had peeped out of the window, she had seen the Rolls in the street below.

Nothing in her serene appearance gave any indication of her delight at seeing him as she replied to his good morning. She got into the car and asked without preamble: 'Why did you want to see me—it is my day off . . .'

He ignored this. 'Are you coming to Holland with us?'

She was being rushed; of course she would go, the prospect of spending a week in his company, even if surrounded by boys and presumably, his fiancée, was one not to be missed. But she hadn't intended to tell him so soon, he might think she was eager . . . She said baldly: 'Yes.'

'Splendid. We shall go—let me see, on the seventeenth and come back on the twenty-first. Can you manage that?'

'Well, I think so—I'll get all the Christmas arrangements fixed up before then; Pat won't mind—and we can get the actual decorations and extra food and things done easily a couple of days before Christmas.'

'Good. We'll drive over—it's quicker in the long run. Bring warm clothes with you.'

He started the car and she said: 'Yes, but that's all settled then, isn't it? There's no need—I've some shopping, and I'm having lunch . . .'

'With me, Julia, and I fancy you've just dreamed up the shopping.'

She had the grace to blush. 'All the same,' she said firmly, 'this won't do. I don't care what you say about colleagues, if I were your fiancée I'd be hopping mad.'

'I should hope you would be. I thought I'd made it clear that we have a deep and mutual regard for each other which nothing—I repeat nothing—can shake. Now shall we leave the subject alone once and for all?'

Julia said meekly, 'Very well.' And in an effort to bring the conversation on to a matter-of-fact plane, 'It isn't a very nice day, is it?'

They were driving towards the West End. 'As regards the weather—no—otherwise I have no quarrel with it.'

She tried again. 'It will soon be Christmas,' and stopped because it was an idiotic thing to say.

The professor must have considered it idiotic as well, for he didn't answer. He was going smoothly through side streets and it wasn't until they were in New Oxford Street that he spoke again. 'You have a passport?'

She stared out at the pavements, packed with shoppers. 'Yes, I have.'

He grunted something and turned into one of the narrow side streets. 'Where are we going?' asked Julia.

'I live near here.'

She kept quiet then while he turned into South Audley Street and then into another narrow street almost at its end. There were small elegant Regency houses on either side and he stopped at the end one.

Julia turned and looked at him. 'You live here?'

He smiled a little. 'Where did you think I lived—or perhaps you never thought about it?'

'Oh, but of course I did,' she said with a frankness which widened his smile. 'Somewhere near St Anne's, though heaven knows where—a service flat where you can eat in the restaurant on the ground floor.'

'That makes me sound very lonely.'

'Well, I thought you were until I met Nicholas.' She added, 'Bad tempered too and dreadfully aloof, only I don't think you are at all. I've always thought you didn't like me, so I took care . . .' She bit her lip, for she had almost given herself away. She ended tamely: 'It's very pleasant here.'

'Very. Come inside.' They got out and crossed the

narrow pavement and he opened his front door and
ushered her inside.

The hall was larger than she had expected it to be,
warmly carpeted in burgundy red, with several doors
leading from it and a gracefully curving staircase
leading to a small gallery above. There was a door
beside the staircase and this opened as they went in
and a woman came to meet them. She had a round
face with blue eyes and iron grey hair screwed into an
old-fashioned bun; the rest of her was round too, her
ample proportions tidily confined in a dark dress and a
print pinafore.

'This is Martha,' said the professor, and as Julia
offered a hand, 'I've brought Sister Mitchell, for
coffee, Martha. Could we have it in the drawing room
presently?'

'Two ticks, Professor. Just let me take the young
lady's coat and show her the cloakroom.'

He nodded rather vaguely, tossed his coat on to a
wall table and opened one of the doors. 'I'll be in
here.'

Julia followed Martha down the hall to a door set
under the stairs.

'Everything you want there, Sister Mitchell. I'll
fetch the coffee.'

Julia took off her beret, did things to her hair and
face and went back into the hall. A door was opened as
she did so. 'In here,' said the professor, and she went
past him into a room which made her catch her breath.
It had windows at each end, draped with heavy silk
curtains in Venetian red, they matched the thick
carpet and made a delightful background for the rich
cream and burgundy covers on the easy chairs and two
sofas on either side of the marble fireplace. Under one

window there was a delicate sofa table, flanked by small chairs upholstered in dark green, and the same green had been used for the cushions on the sofas. Small circular tables held reading lamps with cream silk shades and the bright fire shone and twinkled on the old-fashioned, highly polished brass fender and fire irons.

'Oh, how very nice,' said Julia, 'it's rude to say so, isn't it? But it's so charming.'

'And unexpected?' The professor was watching her with interest.

'Oh, yes.'

'You think that my wife will like it?'

Just for a few moments she had forgotten; his words made her catch her breath but she said steadily. 'I'm quite sure she will, hasn't she seen it yet?'

'No.'

'But it's always been like this?' And when he nodded she looked puzzled. Surely the girl would have come to his home at some time or other. A likely solution struck her. She would be Dutch, living in Holland and very likely not yet been in London. In which case who was the pretty girl she had seen outside the cinema? Curiosity got the better of discretion.

'Then it's not the girl I spoke to that evening—outside the cinema . . .'

He said calmly: 'No it's not, Julia.'

She nodded. 'She's in Holland of course. You'll be seeing her when you go, that'll be nice.'

Nice sounded a bit tepid but he echoed her blandly, 'Very nice. Sit down, here's the coffee.'

It was then that she noticed the small whiskered face peering round his legs. A foxy face with anxious beady eyes. 'Ah, yes,' went on the professor, 'meet

Digby—a little shy of strangers, I'm afraid, owing to a rather fraught puppyhood.'

Julia bent to pat the unruly thatch on the beast's head and was struck by the enormous plume of a tail which waved gently as she tickled one ear.

'He's a dog of character. That's a lovely tail.'

'Much admired. He's quite young, we're not sure exactly how old he is.'

'You found him?'

'I removed him from unpleasant surroundings.'

'Oh—a pond and a brick round his neck?' she cried in horror.

'Something like that. If you sit down I think he'll make friends.'

She went obediently to one of the chairs grouped round the fire. There were two cats on one of the sofas; a splendid Burmese of impeccable pedigree and a moggy in a black and white coat with half an ear and round green eyes. The professor came to sit opposite her. He waved a large hand at the cats. 'Ruby and Minou. They're Nicky's but while he's away they have to put up with me.'

'Ruby seems very suitable—but Minou . . .?'

'There's nothing like a dignified name. Will you pour the coffee?'

An hour passed quickly for Julia. She couldn't remember afterwards what they had talked about but time had flown by, at the end of it Minou had settled on to her knee and Digby had come to nose her gently before taking up position on his master's beautifully polished shoes.

She stirred and smiled across at her host. 'What a lovely way to spend a morning doing nothing,' she observed.

'I must agree and all the better for it being so seldom. How about a walk before lunch?'

They went to Hyde Park, walking briskly across the grass while Digby frisked around them, coming to trot at their heels whenever anyone came too near. And they talked, at least, Julia did most of the talking, forgetful of everything save the delight of feeling completely at ease with someone, while the professor egged her on quietly and listened with a gleam in his eyes which she didn't see.

They turned for home and presently sat down to a delicious lunch, served by a beaming Martha. Soup, hot and fragrant, lamb cutlets with a splendid variety of vegetables, and treacle pudding, light as air and smothered in the rich syrup. They drank hock and had coffee round the fire in the drawing room. Crossing the hall, Julia wished very much that she would be allowed to see the rest of the house; the dining room hadn't disappointed her with its oval table of highly polished yew and its accompanying chairs with their simple sabre legs and upholstered seats. There was a sideboard too in the grecian style with tapering cupboards, and a narrow serving table against the other wall. The walls were panelled and the whole given colour by the sapphire blue curtains at the tall window and the pale apricot silk of the lamp shades. They drank their coffee in a companionable silence and presently she said, 'I must be going. Thank you for having me to lunch, I—I enjoyed it very much.'

The professor put down his cup and saucer. 'I have enjoyed it too. Must you go? You are perhaps bored with my company? I had hoped that you would stay to tea at least?'

'I'm not bored,' she told him forthrightly, 'it's lovely to be able to talk to someone . . .'

'You miss young Longman?'

She shook her head slowly. 'Not any more—just for a day or two but you see he liked to talk over his day's work.' She gave him a questioning look. 'Don't you ever want to talk about your day?'

'Oh, yes, but Nicky is hardly old enough and Martha doesn't believe in what she calls hospital nonsense.'

'Oh, well when you are married you will have your wife to listen to you.'

'I look forward to that. Nicky's mother disliked my work intensely, I suspect that is why she left us.'

Julia turned a horrified face to him. 'Left you? But you said that she had died . . .'

'Very shortly after leaving us. She found us dull stuff, poor woman, and went to America and died within weeks of a virus pneumonia. We did all we could . . .'

It didn't strike her how strange it was that he was letting her see into his private life after years of austere politeness. 'Oh, Lauris, I'm so very sorry. How dreadful for you. And for Nicky.'

'He hardly remembers her. He longs for a mother, though.'

'He deserves the very best.' She added recklessly, 'And so do you.'

He gave her a small mocking smile. 'Why Julia, you sound quite heated.' The smile disappeared. 'You of all people, with no happy future to look forward to at the moment.'

She bent her flushed face over Minou who had crept on to her lap again. 'I really must go. I think I'd like to walk back.'

'My dear girl, it's all of four miles.'

'Well, I'll walk the first part of the way—as far as the British Museum, I can get a bus there, or the Underground.'

'Not the Underground,' he said sharply, 'that's no place for a pretty girl like you.'

She smiled kindly at him. 'Look, I'm not a girl, I'm thirty and I'm not delicate or scared easily.'

'Then may I walk with you? As far as the British Museum, and see you on to a bus?' He spoke lightly, ignoring the plans he had had for a quiet dinner somewhere for the two of them.

'I'd like that.' She put the cat down gently and got up. 'Do you take Digby?'

'No, he doesn't like busy streets and he's had a good walk—I'll take him for a stroll later on.'

They went through the quiet streets and squares, almost empty at that hour of the afternoon, but presently they turned into narrow busy streets running parallel with Oxford Street. It was already growing dark, for the clouds hadn't lifted all day and the wind was cutting.

Julia said apologetically: 'You must think I'm mad, walking in this weather.'

He took her arm. 'No, I don't. You're walking away from something, aren't you, Julia?'

Which was so exactly the truth that she had no answer.

They had turned up what was little more than an alley, so that they could gain Oxford Street and cross into Great Russell Street when they became aware of a good deal of noise and commotion ahead of them. The professor slowed his steps as the street ahead of them filled with people. There was a good deal of shouting and arm waving and the angry rumbling mutter of an ill-tempered crowd. The lane they were in, for it was little more than that, was lined with high brick walls and there were windowless buildings housing who knew what. There was nowhere for them to go and to walk on wouldn't do at all. The professor pushed her gently up against a wall and stood in front of her. 'And don't dare to move,' he advised her.

There was nothing further from her mind; his broad back sheltered her nicely even though she was big, and he was reassuringly calm. The crowd were almost upon them by now, pushing and shoving past them, shouting at them too, although she couldn't hear what they were saying. Whatever it was, however, was bad tempered, and the temper seemed to be getting worse as the crowds progressed. Peeping round a massive shoulder she saw that the crowd was fighting as it swayed and stumbled past and she withdrew her head smartly as a blow was aimed at the professor, who calmly lifted an arm and diverted it without effort. She gave a shiver and his other hand came round to hold her arm for a moment in a reassuring grip. He needed it almost at once, though, to parry another blow.

This is really quite frightening, thought Julia and closed her eyes. She opened them again; if they were going to be knocked down and trampled on then she would be of more use to Lauris if she could see. The comforting thought he would never allow her to be trampled on cheered her considerably so that she didn't notice the rough bricks of the wall she was pressed against and even managed to peep at the men and women streaming past her. They were running now and weren't fighting any more and she saw why almost immediately; the police, solid, unhurried and calm, were at their heels. Minutes later, the crowd had gone and the last of the police. One of the officers had paused to ask if they were all right.

'Quite unhurt, Officer,' the professor assured him. 'What was it? A demonstration of some sort?'

'That's right, sir. A few hotheads started something up and there's always those that join in, half of them don't know what it's all about.'

He saluted smartly, smiled at Julia and went on his way.

'Oh, my goodness,' said Julia. She was pale, so that her green eyes seemed greener than ever. 'That was something, wasn't it? Thank heaven you were here. What would I have done?'

He laughed down at her. 'Gone with them, of course, and slipped away when you had the chance. You're not too crushed?'

'No, I'm fine. You're not hurt?'

He shook his head, and she smiled her relief. She was quite unprepared for his quick, fierce kiss.

Julia closed her eyes, just for a moment the dingy little side street became heaven. But only for a moment, she came sharply to earth again with the professor's brisk, 'No more nonsense about going back to your flat. We're going back home to have tea round the fire, and I shall drive you back after dinner this evening.'

'But,' began Julia, unable to go on with whatever she had meant to say because of the speed at which she was being hauled towards Oxford Street. It was obvious to her that the professor had the bit between his teeth and nothing she could say would remove it. She gave up and skipped and half ran beside him. She could argue with him later.

He was a man to get a taxi at the lift of his finger.

She was urged to get in and sat listening to the cabbie and the professor exchanging pungent views on demonstrations, lawful and unlawful. 'Ain't 'arf bad fer business,' grumbled the cabbie. 'See anything of 'em?'

The professor assured him briefly that he had.

Martha came into the hall as the professor opened his front door.

'Now that's a good thing,' she exclaimed cheerfully, 'there's muffins just out of the oven and a splendid Dundee cake I've no doubt it's as good as the Queen herself could bake.' She eyed Julia's still pale countenance. 'I'll have that coat of yours, Miss, and you go and tidy yourself.' Her manner was so motherly and cosy that Julia felt a strong urge to burst into tears, something she seldom did. She swallowed them back, did as she was bid and then joined the professor in his drawing room where a small table had been drawn up before the fire with the tea tray already upon it. It wasn't until she was eating her second muffin and had re-filled their cups that the professor observed, 'You weren't frightened, Julia?'

She sank her splendid teeth into buttery richness. 'Oh, yes, I was, to begin with, but you were there.'

The professor put down his cup. 'Thank you, Julia.' He smiled slowly and she looked away, reminding herself that he was almost a married man and she would have to be careful.

She said lightly, 'You're large you see.'

'Yes, it does help. Cut the cake, will you? If we don't eat at least a couple of slices I shall have Martha in tears.'

They sat and talked after the tea things had been cleared away, with the cats and Digby lined up between them. It seemed no time at all before the professor said, 'How about a drink before dinner?'

'Are you sure that you want me to stay? I mean, you didn't expect me did you? You may have a date this evening . . .'

'Don't fish,' he told her, 'but set your mind at rest, I have no date. Occasionally I have a day off and I do absolutely nothing.'

'Well, it's very kind of you.' She wrinkled her delightful nose. 'Something smells delicious.'

He laughed. 'I have no doubt Martha has excelled herself.'

Martha had. Avocado pears sharpened by a sauce of her own invention, sole veronique and a pineapple upside down pudding with lashings of cream. Julia put down her empty wine glass and said happily, 'That was gorgeous. I think I must have a greedy nature.'

'Nonsense. I've no patience with women who pick at a chicken bone with a tape measure in their hand, terrified to gain an ounce or two.' He stared across the table at her. 'I like women who look like women.'

He grinned so wickedly at her that she blushed, made aware of her own splendid shape. 'I think I should be going back,' she told him in what she hoped was a cool voice. 'Wellington, you know . . .'

'Of course, but we'll have coffee first, shall we?'

But he made no attempt to delay her once they drank it. And beyond a few commonplace remarks as they drove back, he had little to say. At the flat she hesitated.

'No, I won't come in,' he told her, unerringly reading her thoughts. 'I have some work to do.' He got out and went with her to the door and held it open until she had gone through after wishing him good night and muttering her thanks. Only when he heard her open and then close her own door at the top of the stairs did he close the street door and get back into his car. He didn't drive away at once and Julia, going to draw the curtains, stood for a moment looking down at the Rolls. Everything was moving too fast for her, she thought distractedly. Within a few weeks she and Lauris had become friends, and it wasn't just a casual relationship; it had got out of hand, she was so completely at ease with him and she was in danger of forgetting that she knew he was shortly to be married— to a woman who probably thought of her as his working colleague. Which of course she was, or had been. She thought back with wonder to the time when she had found him austere and stand offish. It would be nice, she thought wistfully, if she could have got herself back to that state again. There wasn't any going back now though, she loved him and that was that. She wasn't a woman to accept second best; she would have to remain unmarried and make the best of it. She watched the car draw away from the kerb and then turned away from the window to feed an impatient Wellington and put on the kettle. A cup of tea would hardly alter the situation but at least it made it a little easier to bear.

She was too restless to go to bed; she cleaned the flat and washed her hair and then sat with the kitten on her knee, doing nothing until she glanced at the clock and saw that it was almost midnight. She was on duty at eight o'clock in the morning and there were two lumbar punctures, a couple of barium meals and the physiotherapists would be steaming on to the ward, very bright and cheeful, to instil movement and hope into the more helpless of the patients. She went to bed then, trying to pin her thoughts down to tomorrow's work, a hopeless task as they reverted time and again to Lauris. And when she did sleep at last it was to dream of him.

CHAPTER EIGHT

THE day was even busier than she had expected it to be. Both women for barium meals, took exception to the mixture they were asked to swallow and were, from their point of view, most satisfactorily sick and had to be put back into their beds and the lumbar punctures, although successfully performed by Dick, needed the services of a nurse, ill spared, what with days off and the mopping up which had to be done for the other two patients. Julia went to and fro, managing as best she could, lending a hand here and there, finding time to stop and have a word with some of the more querulous ladies. She looked calm and capable and unhurried. All the same Dick asked her as he swallowed a quick cup of coffee in her office. 'What's up, Julia? You look as though you haven't slept at all?'

'Well, one gets the odd bad night,' she tried to sound casual and achieved a small smile. 'The ward's busy and I suppose I let it prey on my mind too much.'

'That's not like you. Perhaps you need another holiday.' He spoke jokingly.

'I'm going to have one—I'm going over to Holland with my brothers and Professor van der Wagema's son as soon as they start school holidays.'

'Sounds great. Whereabouts in Holland?'

'Friesland. I can't remember the name though.'

'Well, send me a post card.' He got up and prepared

to leave. 'Let me know if that B.P. goes any higher, will you? You're on this weekend?'

She nodded. 'It's take in, too, you'll be in?'

'Yes, the professor's away for a few days.'

His news made the day longer than it really was. And the succeeding days until Thursday seemed endless too; she went on duty uncertain as to whether she would see him. Dick could have told her, of course, but he hadn't, and she hadn't asked. She took the night report with her usual calm unflurried air, sent the night nurse off duty, conferred with Pat as to the day's work and did her usual round, making sure everything was just so; even if the professor wasn't coming, Dick would be, and he was entitled to as much perfection as his chief expected and got.

At ten o'clock precisely the door opened and the professor walked in, gave her a severe good morning, mentioned that he was rather pressed for time and began his round. It went smoothly, with a minimum of talk, although she had to admit in all fairness that he allowed no hint of haste to reach his patients. Julia passed forms, X-rays, notes, offered information when asked for it and beyond that said not a word. She was conscious of bitter disappointment; she had thought that their friendship was firmly established, but although he had glanced at her once or twice it was with a detached air, as though he couldn't quite remember who she was and did it matter anyway. The last patient dealt with, she led the way through the ward door held open by a student nurse, and paused on the landing outside her office. Perhaps after all the professor would change his mind and have coffee, although she wasn't going to ask him. But he merely handed the notes he was carrying to Dick, wished her a polite good morning, and walked off, followed by Dick and his usual cortege of students.

Julia, extremely cross, flounced into the office, thumped the notes on to her desk and sat down. But she couldn't gloom for long; Pat came in with the coffee tray, remarking cheerfully that the professor had seemed to be more wintry than usual. 'Rumour has it that he's getting married soon—I pity his poor wife. He looked as though he wanted to tear you apart.'

She poured their coffee. 'I've sent the two students to coffee. Nurse Fell's on the ward with the second year nurse. They're tidying up.'

Julia nodded absently. What had she done to merit the black looks and chilly manner? The answer popped into her head almost at once. He'd been to Holland and had a row with his fiancée, perhaps because he may have told her that he had entertained his ward sister at his home for no valid reason. Julia's cheeks grew hot at the very idea. Well, serve him right if the girl had given him the sharp edge of her tongue; she would have done the same. She felt real sympathy for her; she might love the wretched man to distraction herself, but that was neither here nor there; she had no right to him and this girl had. 'I'll not go to Holland,' she muttered out loud.

Pat asked in surprise, 'Holland? Were you thinking of going there?'

Julia said hurriedly: 'Oh, I had some idea—but I don't think I will.' She was losing her grip if this was what love did to you, the quicker she put several hundred miles between her and Lauris the better. Pat was still looking questioningly at her.

'It would be too near Christmas, I'd only have four or five days when I got back . . .'

'But that's heaps of time. We could get the ward presents before you go—it'll be easier for one thing, and if you make out the lists for the food and so on, I can hand them in while you're away. If you know what you'd like for decorations this year, we can get some of the convalescent ladies to make a start. You know how they always enjoy that.'

It was all being made so easy for her. Julia took a sip of coffee. 'Well, yes, it could be done, I suppose. Even if I don't go, we might get the presents bought. We'd better pick on something cheerful this year. The ward's full of patients who won't be going home for several weeks and there are bound to be more in before Christmas.'

'Why don't we have tulips and windmills and Dutch figures. A compliment to the professor. I've just thought, Sister, do you want to collect for a wedding present?'

Julia went a little pale, but her voice was steady enough. 'Well, that's a difficulty—I mean are we supposed to know that he's getting married? He's never told us,' the pallor became pink, 'I mean not officially. He might be peeved, thinking his private life had been invaded.'

Pat took another biscuit. 'I bet he's quite something—away from this place, I mean. A bit old, of course.'

A hot denial was on Julia's lips, repressed just in time. Of course, from Pat's youthful twenty-two, he must seem almost middle-aged. But just right for me, said Julia silently to herself, and really she must try and stop thinking nonsense like that and remember that poor trusting girl in Holland. She frowned into her mug. Although the professor had done nothing he need be ashamed of; it was natural to be on good terms with the people one worked with added to the fact that a sensible girl wouldn't object to that. She knew she herself would mind very much, she was astonished how het up she got at the very thought of the professor taking any other woman out, however harmlessly. But he wouldn't of course, not without telling her so. She became a little muddled in her thinking and was quite startled when Pat asked, 'Shall I get old Mrs Drew out of bed? Half an hour, Professor van der Wagema said, didn't he?'

Julia dragged her thoughts away from her own affairs and concentrated on Mrs Drew. 'Yes, I'll come with you, just in case she starts something . . .'

They walked into the ward together and spent the next ten minutes coaxing the old lady to sit in a chair. She had been very ill and so sure that she was going to die, that she refused to accept the professor's assurances that she had several useful years ahead of her provided she played her part.

'Just while we make your bed,' cajoled Julia, and lifted her patient into the chair waiting for her. And after half an hour lifted her back, just in time for her dinner. 'There, that wasn't too bad, was it?' asked Julia. 'And Professor van der Wagema will be so pleased when he comes next week.'

She sailed down the ward to the dinner trolley and began to dole out diets. Diabetics, fat frees, high proteins, low residues; there were never more than half a dozen patients eating a normal plateful. She, who ate everything and anything with a healthy appetite, pitied the recipients of steamed fish and creamed chicken, so many ounces of ham and a precise cube of bread. She took trouble to arrange the food nicely on the plates and made sure that it was hot. The nurses who worked for her liked her, but agreed among themselves that when it came to meal times on the ward she could be something of a martinet.

Before she went off duty that evening, she gathered all the nurses in her office while Pat kept an eye on the ward, so that she could explain about Christmas and the preparations involved. 'Staff and I will shop for patients' presents quite soon, perhaps next week, and if any of you have some ideas about what to buy do please tell me. We wondered if we had a Dutch scene for decorations this year—we can get some of the patients on to making paper flowers and if any of you can draw and paint we could do with a few windmills and Dutch girls in clogs. Do you like the idea?'

They chorused agreement and she promised to have another meeting after the presents were bought. 'For I'll want volunteers to wrap parcels,' she warned them. 'I shan't get much money from the office so keep ideas down to round about a pound for each patient! It would mean digging into her own pocket, of course, it always did, but she didn't mind that, there would be small gifts for the nurses too and something extra for Pat who was hoping to get engaged in a few months. And food—the hospital supplied the basics but she would buy the extras. The professor, in time-honoured custom, provided them with drinks and as always, would hand her something impersonal like a handsome diary, which she never used—or a note case, or occasionally, a book token. And she and the nurses in their turn would give him something equally impersonal. He'd had a pen last year—perhaps a propelling pencil. He must have dozens; hers wasn't the only ward where he had patients—there were

Women's Medical, Children's, Out Patients, Private Patients, all in honour bound to exchange something useless with him.

She went off duty and over her supper made several lists in her neat handwriting. There was really not all that hurry to do them, but they kept her busy, and if she was busy she didn't think about Lauris, at least not so much. But lists couldn't last for ever. Once she was in bed her thoughts centred on him. And the more she thought the crosser she became. There he was, spending a day with her on the friendliest of terms, and being utterly charming and yet this morning he had behaved as though he had no interest in her whatsoever, other than as his ward sister.

She gave Wellington's ears a tweak. 'I shall not go to Holland,' she told him firmly.

She was still of the same mind the next morning, and indeed throughout the day, buoyed up by sad, romantic thoughts in which Lauris appeared most satisfactorily as a man shaken by remorse, begging her pardon in a most abject fashion while she turned her back on St Anne's and took a job in some Godforsaken spot thousands of miles away. The sensible side of her mind told her that she was indulging in silly daydreams more suited to a teenager but since she was deriving some comfort from these, she chose to ignore common sense for once. Even a night's sleep didn't quite dispel them and she went on duty the next day, ready to be brought out when she had a moment to herself. Not that there were many moments. Pat had a weekend and there was more than enough to keep her busy but there was a lull after lunch, while the patients had their visitors and the nurses were doing odd jobs in the linen room or the sluice with one eye on the ward. She herself would go out presently and walk through the ward so that friends and relations could buttonhole her and ask questions. But it was too early for that; she began on the paper work and had her head bent over the off duty list when the door opened and the professor walked in.

It annoyed her very much that she should colour up so easily. She said coldly: 'You wanted to see someone, sir?' and she stood up.

'You, Julia.' He put out a hand and pushed her gently back into her chair.

Her eyes glinted greenly. She said quite unforgivably, for no Sister would speak to a senior consultant in such a fashion: 'I'm busy.'

He sat himself down on the edge of the desk and bent over to see her lists; she had been doodling too—a dog, very like Digby and a pair of cats. She snapped the books shut and laid them precisely over her drawings, then looked up at him.

He picked out the off-duty book without haste, opened it at the page she had been writing in, took out his pen and scrawled something across it.

'Well, really,' said Julia, much affronted and snatched the book to see what he'd written. Under the week beginning December 17th he had written 'holidays' beside her name. 'In any case, I have decided not to go.'

'Yes, I thought that you might, that's why I came, though heaven knows it's most inconvenient. Tell me why aren't you coming?'

It was difficult to put into words. She sat silent for a few moments staring down at the off-duty book—she would have to tear the page out. At length she said slowly, 'I did mean to come with you all—I wanted to meet your fiancée,' a lie if ever there was one, but it sounded right, somehow. 'But I think it wouldn't do. One day I'm Julia and—and we're friends, and then the next morning ...' She sighed deeply without knowing it, 'I thought that we aren't friends at all—when you did the round you looked at me as though you could not stand the sight of me—very austere and horribly polite you were, looking down your long nose.'

'What would you say if I came on to the ward and said "Hullo, Julia" and kissed the top of your delightful nose and suggested that I came round for coffee later that evening?'

She was horrified. 'You wouldn't—I'd want the floor to open and swallow me.'

He said silkily: 'There's your answer, Julia.' Then his voice was stern, 'So you will come with us, let us have no more prissy nonsense.'

'Prissy,' she almost choked over the word. 'For two pins I'd ...'

'No, no, don't start again.' He laughed a little. 'Do you find me very tiresome, Julia?'

'Yes—no. I'm sure it makes no difference what I think.' She said peevishly.

'No, it doesn't.' He got up. 'I'm on my way to see Nicky, he'll be delighted that you will be joining us. I'll let you know the details in good time.' At the door he turned. 'Do you still think of Longman?'

He'd already asked her that, she remembered. 'Yes, but it doesn't matter anymore.'

He nodded. 'I'll be in on Tuesday as usual, unless something urgent turns up.'

Julia sat at her desk, her lists forgotten, going over everything he had said. She didn't feel any wiser.

And certainly she had no further clue on Tuesday; the round went precisely as it always did. The professor was politely aloof but everlastingly patient with the twenty-four women under his care, behaving just as he always did, only after ten minutes' polite conversation over coffee when he had finished, did he turn and smile at Julia from the door. It was a smile to melt her insides, tender, amused, and faintly wicked.

She had planned to go home on the following weekend but before then she had an afternoon off duty and since Pat had a half day, they chose to go shopping. Their lists had been carefully compiled; the nurses had been helpful, it was just a question of finding the things on the list and buying them. Between them they were more or less successful, even after a quick cup of tea there was half an hour to spare. Dick Reed was easy; he was a great reader when he had the time and the latest thriller was on the book shelves. It remained for them to think of something for the professor.

'Something for his home?' suggested Pat, 'I mean, if he's going to get married he might be glad of some ornaments . . .'

Julia, remembering the rare porcelain and lovely old silver in the drawing room, thought not. 'We gave him a diary last year, didn't we? And the year before that it was a pen. Look, we've still got half an hour if we take a taxi back. Let's try in Liberty's.'

Ten minutes later, in the picture department, she stopped in front of a small water colour. It depicted a canal, peaceful between water meadows, with a windmill in the distance, a few trees and cows grazing peacefully. It was exactly right, simple and without the touch of genius but it would find a place on the professor's walls and wouldn't look out of place. The price was shocking, but Pat, unaware of it's cost, agreed that it was perfect.

'It's a bit more than we meant to pay,' said Julia carefully, 'but we could give it to him as a wedding present, couldn't we, as well as something for Christmas.'

'What a good idea. Shall I take it to the cash desk?'

'No, I'll take it while you get some of that wrapping paper and some labels.'

It was ridiculous to spend so much money, she would have to go without the new sweater she had planned to buy to take to Holland, and she would have to get something for Nicholas too.

She went home at the weekend, to find Nicholas there, delighted to see her. Of his father there was no sign, and no one mentioned him until she did, while she was out in the paddock, grooming Star and Jane.

'I expect you'll see more of your father when you're holidaying?' she observed, carefully casual.

'Oh, rather, he's in Holland this weekend, otherwise he'd have been down to see me. He comes whenever he can, only he said this was an important family matter, to do with him getting married, he said.'

'Oh, yes?' said Julia faintly. 'I expect you're looking forward to having a mother?'

'You bet I am.' He lifted one of Jane's hooves and inspected it carefully. 'Did you like our home? Father told me you'd spent a day there.'

'Oh, did he?' Julia made a great effort to stay casual. 'Yes, I thought it was quite super. And I loved the animals.'

The boy beamed at her. 'Smashers aren't they? But I like Wellington too.'

The talk veered towards cats and dogs and horses and the professor wasn't mentioned again. Julia wasn't sure whether to be pleased or sorry about that.

The professor did his usual round on Tuesday without, however, vouchsafing any information about his absence. Not that she had expected any. They exchanged the usual small talk over coffee and she watched his large frame disappear down the corridor with some annoyance . . . she had hardly expected him to discuss his weekend with her, but he could have mentioned Nicholas; he must have known that she had been with the boy over the weekend. She got on with the day's work feeling put out and headachy. The headache got worse as the day wore on and by the evening when she got to the flat, she knew she was in for a cold.

She spent the next day fighting it off and then, urged by Pat, she took to her bed, crawling out of it to see to Wellington, make endless pots of tea, and take another dose of panadol.

It was midday on the second day when there was a knock on the door and in answer to her gruff come in, the professor entered.

Julia took one look at him, closed her eyes, and said weakly. 'Oh, no . . .'

He put his case down on the table and came to sit on the edge of the divan. 'My poor girl. Pat told me you were off sick.' He took her wrist and checked her pulse and studied her face with its red nose and puffy eyes. 'When did you last eat?' he asked.

'Ugh,' muttered Julia. 'I'm not hungry.'

He got off the bed and went to open his case. 'Take these now . . .' He fetched water and watched while she swallowed pills obediently. 'And now a cup of tea and then food. Is there any soup in your cupboard?'

'Yes, but please don't bother, I'm not hungry; I'll get something presently.'

He took no notice at all, she could have saved her breath. She sat in bed watching him dealing with the soup, making the tea and then because he was fussing, feeding Wellington. She drank her tea and then, reluctantly, the soup.

'Every drop,' said the professor inexorably and when she had finished fetched a basin, added drops to boiling water, draped a towel over her head, and bade her inhale the fumes until he told her she could stop.

'Bully,' muttered Julia, and heard him laugh.

'I'll have you up on your feet if it kills me,' he told her. 'Why in heaven's name didn't you get your doctor?'

Her voice came muffled from under the towel. 'You are my doctor.' She sneezed. 'The nursing staff are allowed the consultants you know.' She sneezed again. 'Don't tell me you weren't aware of that.'

'Of course, I'm aware. Recollect if you can that doctors don't usually offer their services until they are requested.'

She lifted a corner of the towel. 'Then why are you here? I don't want a doctor for a cold in the head.'

'No, but Women's Medical need Sister back on duty.'

'I'll be back tomorrow.'

'You dare.' His voice was equable and at the same time very firm. 'You will stay here for another twenty-four hours. I shall visit you tomorrow and if you are fit enough you may return on the following day.'

Her peevish retort was swallowed up in a mighty

sneeze and all he did was to laugh gently, pat her
shoulder in a sympathetic manner and go away.

He didn't come again until the evening of the next day
and by then she was feeling much better. She had taken
the pills he had left for her, and eaten the meals her
landlady had laboured up the stairs to bring her, rather
taken aback at that lady's kindness until she discovered
that the professor had exerted his charm upon her, and
his charm, when he bothered with it, was considerable.

She was in her dressing gown, sitting by the gas fire
when he came and he said at once: 'Ah, better, I see.
Good, Pat wanted to come and see you but I advised
her not to, there was no point in her catching your
cold. How do you feel?'

He put his case down and took her pulse and told
her to put out her tongue. 'You're on at one o'clock
tomorrow, aren't you? Well, go on duty and see how
you feel at the end of the day. Now don't be silly, if
you don't feel the thing by the evening, take another
day off. Promise?'

She nodded. 'I'm perfectly all right, thank you.'

'Yes, I know you are,' he said with heavy patience,
'that's why I said that you might go back tomorrow.
You'll have Pat there until the evening and she knows
what to do.'

Julia shot him a green glance. 'I'm quite able to run
my ward, Professor.'

'Yes, yes, don't get all worked up. I should have
said that she will know what to do if you don't feel
quite the thing.'

Julia mumbled sorry and anxious to make amends,
offered tea.

'A good idea. I'll make it. Nicky is very anxious
about you.'

'Nicky? Is he? He is a dear boy—I like him. Please tell him that I'm fine and looking forward to seeing him.'

'I have 'phoned your mother . . .'

Julia turned a surprised face to his. 'Did you? That was kind, I was going to ring her this evening.'

'Well, you still can, although I can't see the sense of traipsing down that draughty staircase and catching another cold. Can't you 'phone from your office tomorrow?'

'You must know,' she told him severely, 'that nursing staff aren't allowed to use the ward 'phones.'

'Well, of course I know.' He handed her a cup of tea. 'But don't tell me that the rule isn't broken.'

'Well, perhaps, just now and then.' She tossed back her red mane. 'All right I'll wait until tomorrow.' She remembered something. 'And thank you for asking my landlady to bring me meals. How on earth did you ever persuade her? She's a good landlady as they go, I suppose, but she believes in keeping oneself to oneself at all times.'

'So I should imagine. Shall I wash your hair for you?'

She goggled at him. 'Wash my . . .? I'm going to do it before I go to bed. Does it look awful then?'

'You have very beautiful hair and it doesn't look awful, well—not too awful. You always keep it clean and shining.'

She cast about for a suitable answer to this and could think of none. The professor watching her, smiled a little. 'What will you do with Wellington while we are away?'

'Take him home. I've a day off in the week before we go. He'll be quite happy with Gyp and the cats.

It's much more fun for him there; with a garden and more room.'

He agreed gravely, put down his cup and prepared to go. He said, suddenly smooth: 'I've a date this evening, I shall be late if I don't go now. Take care of yourself and finish the pills, won't you?'

'Thank you for coming,' said Julia sedately, wondering furiously who the date was with. Perhaps his fiancée had come back with him if he'd been in Holland. She longed to ask but instead uttered a polite good night. The room felt very empty when he'd gone.

She felt so much better the next morning that she spent it cleaning the flat, getting groceries from the corner shop and taking extra pains with her appearance. Her hair, smooth and shining once more, she pinned up as she always did, but with time on her hands, she spent ages over her face. A silly thing to do actually. Lauris wouldn't be at the hospital and he hadn't mentioned seeing her again, but there was always the faint hope . . .

So faint that by the time she was ready to go off duty that evening, it had died. She had been busy; the ward was full and there were things to catch up with; things Pat had left for her to do, and there were several new patients to see. She was tired by eight o'clock and glad to hurry through the wintry, bleak streets and climb the stairs to her flat.

Wellington, without company after a couple of days of having her all to himself, fell about with pleasure at the sight of her and then gobbled his supper and fell instantly asleep. Julia yawned widely. 'Bed,' she observed to the unconscious beast, 'but I suppose I must make some supper first.'

She was a good housewife and there was plenty in her small store cupboard, but the prospect of having to cook wasn't inviting. She was trying to decide between soup and toasted cheese when someone knocked on the door. Supper, she thought hopefully, perhaps her landlady was still feeling the effects of Lauris's charm?

She called come in and the professor opened the door.

'I had intended to be here by the time you got back,' he told her without wasting time on a hullo, 'but circumstances prevented me.'

He put a cardboard box on the table. 'I've brought our supper: I'm sure you don't feel well enough to go out.'

Julia stood with her mouth slightly agape, staring at him. 'Supper?' she asked like an idiot. 'I was just going to toast some cheese . . .'

'Throw it out of the window.' He lifted out a thermos and a couple of plastic containers. 'Put a cloth on the table there's a good girl,' he begged.

They sat down presently opposite each other, the professor as matter-of-fact as though he was in the habit of calling on people and bringing his food with him; Julia in a bit of a daze because it was all rather unexpected.

The soup was delicious—'Martha's best,' commented Lauris, and the cold chicken and salad were superb. 'And where on earth did you get strawberries at this time of year?' Julia wanted to know. She hadn't known that she was hungry; she ate everything put before her while her companion kept up a trickle of light conversation.

Over coffee presently, she thanked him. 'And I

can't think why you take so much trouble,' she finished.

He gave her a level look. 'Nicky is most anxious that you should be quite fit for your visit to Holland,' he told her. Which was somehow a disappointing answer.

He didn't linger once they had finished, but put the remains of their meal back in the box, washed the crockery despite her strong protests, bade her a friendly good night, got into his coat, and left as quickly as he had come.

'The strangest man,' said Julia to the closed door, 'but how I love him.'

She allowed herself ten minutes' day dreaming, and then, telling herself that she was a fool to waste her time, went to bed.

She was still young, and healthy with it; she was back into the routine of the ward by the next day and by the time the professor did his next round she was her usual calm self, giving proper answers to his questions, her mind bent on the task in hand and later on, as she and Dick and the professor drank their coffee, she discussed the Christmas preparations in a matter-of-fact way; she had them all organised by now; there was nothing much more to be done, she would be able to go away for a few days knowing that everything was in train. Of course, she had no intention of telling him that they were transforming the ward into a Dutch scene; those women who were able were already making paper flowers and the most junior of the student nurses had turned out to be quite an artist. He would see it all when he arrived on Christmas morning to carve the turkey.

The days slid by, and Julia, immersed in work, hardly noticed them passing. The weather had turned cold with a sullen wind and grey skies and an occasional downpour of rain. Hardly the weather for a holiday she thought, catching a train home with Wellington in his basket. She was going for the day; her other free day she intended adding on to her leave so that she would have the leisure to pack and do her nails and hair and stock up her cupboard ready for Christmas. She wouldn't be going home again until the very end of the year and she had the presents for the family with her.

Her mother was having a baking day; the boys would be home for Christmas and Madge and Jim and little Harry would be there too. 'A pity you can't get home, love,' observed Mrs Mitchell, 'we'll have to make up for that later. Will you be free at all?'

'An hour or two, Mother, but I can't count on it. It's Pat's turn to be off this year and the nurses each have one free day. But there's plenty to do on the ward, you know and the other nurses come visiting to see the decorations . . .'

'Yes, dear,' persisted her mother, 'but when you go back to that little flat of yours you'll be alone.'

'I'll have Wellington and I daresay I'll be glad to be quiet and that I shan't mind at all.' She spoke cheerfully, aware that she would be very lonely indeed, thinking of Lauris, cosily sitting by his fire in his lovely house, with Nicky to keep him company and the animals and Martha in the kitchen cooking some delicacy. She ate a mince pie from the plateful her mother had put on the table and when she was asked, said that yes, she was quite ready to go on holiday.

'The boys are so excited. Where are you meeting everyone?'

Julia took a bite of pie. 'I don't know. I expect Lauris will tell me. He's one of those peope who arrange everything and then lets you know at the last minute.'

She went back to her flat in the evening, laden with presents from the family and with a batch of mince pies. Without Wellington the flat seemed very inhospitable.

It wasn't until the day before she was to go on holiday that Lauris at the end of his round told her casually to be ready at seven o'clock. 'That will give you time to change after duty,' he pointed out unnecessarily. 'We'll wait outside the flat. We're going on the Harwich night ferry.'

He had gone before she could frame a single question.

CHAPTER NINE

JULIA had hoped to get off duty punctually so that she would have time to do everything at her ease; she had had to scrap her day off because one of the part-time staff nurses was off sick. Luckily she had had the forethought to put everything ready to pack before she had gone on duty that morning. She almost ran to the flat when at last she got off the ward; she had an hour which was better than nothing but she had meant to be ready with time to spare so that by the time the car came for her she would be at her best. As it was, rather red in the face from running and then too hot a shower, she packed a rather nice wool crepe dress the colour of her eyes, slacks, a couple of thick sweaters and blouses and a pair of very expensive shoes about which she had always felt guilty but now felt justified in buying; they went so well with the dress. She had already filled her good leather handbag with her passport, some Dutch money, her cheque book and an asssortment of useful odds and ends; safety pins, snaps of her baby nephew, a lucky charm she wouldn't have dreamt of leaving behind, a pocket screw driver Jason had given her for some reason or other and of course her make-up. It only remained for her to put on her tweed suit and a cashmere jumper, ram the velvet beret on her head, put her thick gloves and quilted jacket ready by her case and go to the window to watch for the Rolls.

It was already there, a minute or two early, and she

picked up her things and made for the door. Lauris
was on the landing. He took her case from her, said:
'Good girl,' kissed her swiftly and led the way
downstairs. Julia following him, thought crossly, that
he never gave her the chance to say anything. If she
had managed to get a good evening in first, it might
have stopped him kissing her. On reflection, she was
glad that she had no opportunity to speak.

The three boys were in the back of the Rolls. They
were in the highest of spirits and getting into the car
she was greeted with shouts of pleasure as the
professor stowed her in the front seat and then went
back to put her case in the boot.

They were all talking at once when he came back
and it seemed that he shared their good spirits for they
were all laughing and talking as he drove off. Julia
wondered briefly what she had let herself in for.

The professor drove steadily through the East End,
through Ilford and Romford and Brentwood and then
on to Chelmsford and thence to Colchester and the
road to Harwich. But before they reached that town
the professor stopped outside a Happy Eater roadside
café and ushered them all inside for coffee. It was
warm inside, the air was flavoured with frying bacon
and chips and the three boys looked hungry. The
professor came back with a tray of coffee and Gregory,
who'd gone with him to help, bore a plate of
doughnuts, which the boys devoured like young
wolves. Julia, who hadn't eaten much all day found
her mouth watering and was relieved when the
professor observed that they would have dinner just as
soon as they got on board.

They went on their way again presently and,
shepherded through Customs and out of the car in the

ship's garage, they were conducted to their cabins. 'The dining room in fifteen minutes,' the boys were reminded as they were left at their cabin door. And a moment later outside her own cabin: 'Can you be ready in five minutes? Meet me in the bar, we'll have a drink before we're overwhelmed.'

It was amazing what one could do in the space of five minutes to improve one's person. Julia found her way to the bar with a few seconds to spare and found Lauris already there. 'Sherry?' he asked her as she settled on a stool beside him.

She nodded happily; tomorrow she wouldn't be so happy; she would meet the girl he was going to marry and her heart would break. She had been a fool to come she supposed, but on the other hand she wanted to see what kind of a girl he had chosen.

'You're thinking dire thoughts,' said Lauris gently. 'We are, after all, on holiday, you know.'

She lifted her glass. 'Not dire at all. Here's to a delightful day or two. The boys are beside themselves, aren't they?'

He nodded. 'You'll be worn out by the time we come back; they have so many plans I doubt if we will get to bed at all; there'll be no time.'

'I'm not sure just where we're going . . .'

'Friesland—in the north. Near Leeuwarden. A village near some lakes. I think you'll like it.'

'Is it like your home in London?'

'Not in the least.'

He didn't add to that so she said presently: 'Nicky said that you had a cottage near Winchester . . .'

'We go there a good deal in the summer when I can get away—I fetch him on a Sunday from school. It's small and isolated and quite delightful. He has a pony there. There's a farm not far away, the daughter of the house looks after the cottage and the pony when we're away. I dare say it will get used a good deal more often when I'm married.'

'Your—your fiancée likes the country?'

'Oh yes. Shall we find the boys?'

A gentle snub. She accompanied him to the restaurant and they found the three boys looking famished. They hadn't quite finished their meal when the ship sailed and there was an instant request that they should go on deck.

'Please, Father,' begged Nicholas. 'Julia is dying to go, aren't you, Julia?'

She said instantly: 'I can't wait. Could we come back for our coffee? We wouldn't stay long would we?'

They trooped on deck to stand briefly in the cold to watch the Essex coast fade into the dark, and at the professor's quiet word went back again.

Julia, followed them thankfully, for it had been icy outside, heard the professor murmur in her ear. 'What a splendid mother you will make, Julia. I can see you playing cricket while the dinner burns.'

She laughed with a sad heart, because his words had conjured up a pleasant picture of several little Laurises wielding cricket bats while their father bowled.

It was a rough crossing but she was too tired to mind that. She slept soundly and joined the boys and the professor for breakfast, instantly drawn into a discussion as to the exact distance they would have to drive.

It was a cold dark morning but that made no difference to the good spirits of the party. They were very excited, the boys, the professor quietly pleased to be in his own country and Julia just happy to be sitting beside him again as he nosed the car away from the customs shed and started north.

The professor sent the Rolls surging ahead, bypassing Den Haag and Amsterdam, taking the motorway to Alkmaar. The boys talked non-stop, asking endless questions which he answered with patient good humour. Julia was quiet, a prey to mixed feelings, and he, after a quick glance at her face, said nothing.

Just south of Alkmaar he took a side road, winding between water meadows and running through widely scattered villages, and presently drew up outside a large hotel restaurant set back from the road among trees. The boys needed no second bidding to get out and went ahead, leaving Julia and Lauris to follow.

They went up the path together, his arm tucked in hers. 'We're almost on the Afsluitdijk,' he told her, 'another hour or so and we'll be home.' He didn't tell her more than that and anyway there wasn't much chance; the boys were already sitting at a table in the comfortable restaurant and impatient for their coffee. The talk became animated as they drank the fragrant brew and the boys, always hungry, ate *Kaas broodjes* as they tossed plans, half of which they would never have the time to carry out, to and fro across the table. But they didn't linger; half an hour later they were on their way again to the great sluices which led them on to the twenty-mile long dyke connecting North Holland with Friesland.

The road ahead of them was almost empty, with the high wall of the dyke shutting out the sea on one side, and on the other the Ijsselmeer, dull and grey in the reluctant light of morning. But the paucity of the view did nothing to dampen the boy's high spirits; indeed, by the time they reached land again Nicholas was singing the Friese National Anthem and trying to make Jason and Gregory sing it too. The professor obligingly translated it for Julia's benefit.

'Frisian blood, rise up and boil,' he explained gravely with a twinkle in his dark eyes.

'How very rousing! Is Nicky singing in Dutch?'

'No, in the Friesian Language. If you look at the signposts, you'll see that the names are written in both Dutch and Friesian.'

She looked obediently out of the window at a passing signpost and naturally enough couldn't make head or tail of it.

They turned away from the main road once they had reached the mainland on to a motorway which ran down the Ijsselmeer coast to Bolsward, where Lauris turned away from the town to take narrow country roads, some of them of brick and running along dykes. The land was flat and open but there were clumps of trees here and there, and large prosperous looking farms. There was a glimpse of water from time to time and Nicky said excitedly: 'We skate there if it's cold enough, Julia, and in the summer we sail. Can you sail a boat?'

'If I had someone to show me how,' Julia told him. 'Of course, you can.'

'Rather—Father taught me—so he'll teach you.'

If only he would, but that was something which belonged to her day dreams. She said cheerfully, 'Not in this weather, I hope,' and the boys rocked with laughter at her little joke. But they were in the mood to laugh at anything. She peeped at Lauris but his profile was calm and a little stern. She hoped that he wasn't vexed with Nicky.

'Are we nearly there?' she asked. She looked around her. 'I like this country, it must be heavenly in the summer.'

The professor didn't answer her but Nicky did, 'Yes it is—you'll love it, but winter's fun too. Look, you can see the trees round the village.'

Indeed there were trees ahead of them and to the side of the narrow road and red-tiled roofs showing between them, and presently they turned into a narrow brick lane leading to the trees, past a cluster of farms and into a tiny village square with its church and circle of cottages, and out of the square on the other side for a bare minute's drive before they turned in between big stone posts and into a drive between a thick border of trees and shrubs. The drive bent in a sharp curve and the house came into view. Only it wasn't a house, it was a small castle with pepper pot towers, brightly painted shutters at the windows and funny little windows in its steep roof.

The professor stopped and the boys tumbled out, followed more slowly by Julia and him. They mounted the double steps with their wrought iron railing and found the splendid door open and a short stout man standing by it.

'Beeker,' said the professor warmly and wrung the man's hand. 'This is Miss Mitchell—Julia, this is Beeker, our friend and mainstay—he runs this place and has done for more years than I care to remember.'

Julia shook hands and was conscious of being looked over, very pleasantly, by a pair of bright blue eyes. 'Delighted Miss,' said Beeker in gruff English, and then spoke to Lauris.

She was conscious of his hand on her arm. 'They are already with my mother, the boys,' he told her and walked across the hall to a big double door left slightly open. It was a splendid hall, the walls hung with paintings and a variety of rather nasty looking weapons, but there were a couple of very comfortable arm chairs on either side of an enormous wall table bearing a gilt clock and some rather hideous candlesticks and the large rug half covering the black-and-white tiles was old and faded, its colours only slightly dimmed by time.

The room they entered was large, with tall narrow windows and a hooded fireplace in which a fire roared invitingly. The furniture here was old too, shining with polish and the chairs covered in brocades and scattered with velvet cushions. The boys were clustered round a chair drawn up to the hearth, but they parted as Julia and Lauris went in and the chair's occupant got up and came to meet them.

The professor's mother was tall; as tall as Julia. She was a big woman who held herself well, and her white hair crowned what must have been a beautiful face in her youth. She was good looking still and dressed, Julia noted, very fashionably. She looked austere but there was nothing austere in her greeting of her son and the look she bent on Julia was full of warmth. 'My dear, I have been looking forward to meeting you—Lauris has told me so much . . . we must get to know each other as quickly as possible.'

Julia agreed politely. She liked the lady on sight but she wasn't likely to see her again after this brief stay and there would be no need to become too friendly? Perhaps she hadn't quite meant it; after all, she was speaking another language, although it sounded faultless enough to Julia's ear.

'I'll get Nel to take you to your room, my dear, but don't stop to unpack. We'll have coffee and then the boys can explore for a while before we lunch.'

'Nel is Beeker's daughter,' said Lauris, 'she'll be in the hall, waiting for you.' He took her hand and they went out of the room together and there sure enough was a plump young woman who beamed at the professor, shook his hand and then shook hands with Julia.

'And if you are wondering what she is saying it is just her name,' explained Lauris. 'It's usual when we're introduced to say our own names at the same time.'

'What a good idea.' Julia wished she could think of something suitable to the occasion; a few words of praise about the smoothness of the journey, a gracefully turned phrase about his mother's welcome. No words came: she stood and stared up into his face, suddenly uncertain about everything and wishing that she had never come.

The professor watched her face from beneath his heavy lids and smiled slowly. He said gently: 'You like my home?'

'Oh, yes.' She was thankful to have been given a lifeline of conversation. 'It's quite beautiful, I had no idea. Don't you wish that you could live here all the time?'

'But one day I shall. It will be Nicky's after me, besides it is such a splendid place in which children may grow up. Until then, I shall live in London and work there too, and come here whenever I can.'

She nodded, spurred on by unhappy thoughts, she asked: 'And your fiancée—she won't mind?'

He gave her a bland smile. 'To tell you the truth, I

haven't yet asked her, but I am sure that she won't have the least objection.'

He glanced at Nel. 'Don't be long; Mother wants to talk to you.'

The staircase was very graceful with shallow stone steps and a wrought iron balustrade topped by gleaming brass rails, it wound up the side of the hall to a circular gallery with doors all round it. Nel opened one of these and ushered Julia inside. It was a beautiful room, overlooking the grounds, which even in winter were a pleasant sight. The window was in a small bay with a sofa table set in it with a mirror on it and a little stool, and the bed had a matching quilt with the chintz curtains and the coverings of the two little arm chairs each side of the fireplace. There were doors along one wall, opening on to a deep closet and a modern bathroom, but there wasn't time to explore them thoroughly. Mindful of Lauris's warning, she did her face, tidied her hair and went back downstairs.

It amazed her to see how at home her two brothers already were; they and Nicky were sitting at a large rent table in one of the window recesses, coffee cups before them and a plate of biscuits which they were sharing with two labradors.

'Come over here by the fire,' said Lauris as she hesitated inside the door, and sat her down in a chair next to his mother before going back to the great winged arm chair he had been sitting in. She was glad of the coffee, it was something to do and she was feeling shy and nervous, although Mevrouw van der Wagema, chattering away about the castle and her daughters and grandchildren, soon put her at her ease.

'I have three sisters,' said Lauris, 'I don't think I've mentioned them.'

'No you haven't, but then, there was no reason for you to do so,' Julia pointed out reasonably, and missed the quick amused glance son and mother exchanged. 'They're married?'

'Oh, yes, and I have five grandchildren, not counting Nicky.' Mevrouw van der Wagema looked positively smug. 'I hope for more.' She beamed at Julia. 'Tell me now, about your family, Julia—you have a sister, do you not?'

Very well informed, thought Julia, she had scarcely thought that Lauris was such a gossip. She obliged with a brief description of her own family and her hostess settled back in her chair. 'Lauris, take the boys away, I wish to talk to Julia.'

The professor got to his feet. 'I'll be back to pour you a drink in half an hour or so,' he told them and wandered off, followed by the boys, much refreshed and ready for any excitement he might have to offer.

'You have known Lauris a long time, my dear?'

Julia shook her head. 'I'm his ward sister, Mevrouw van der Wagema, not a—a friend. At least, not until a month or so ago—he was very kind to me—I was engaged to be married . . .' She skimmed very lightly over the happenings of the last few weeks, not sure that her hostess would be interested, but she was; questions fell thick and fast and it was something of a relief when Lauris reappeared, saying that the boys were in the kitchen plaguing the cook and what would they like to drink?

As he handed Julia her sherry he observed blandly. 'Mother will have wrung you dry, no doubt, but you see she hasn't much time . . .'

Julia wanted to ask why not. Surely his mother wasn't suffering from some incurable complaint?

Perhaps she was going away? Surely not, if he was on the point of getting married. She mumbled and was saved from answering by Mevrouw van der Wagema who wanted to know how Nicky was getting on with his coaching.

They lunched presently, sitting at a vast round table in an impressive room. The table could seat sixteen people and was splendidly decked with starched linen, shining silver and glass and Nel waited at table with Beeker pottering attentively. The food was delicious, and Julia, quite famished, enjoyed every morsel. She shouldn't have done, she told herself silently; people who suffered unrequited love were supposed to go off their food, but so far, she was still as healthily hungry as ever. Eating the mouth-watering apple tart and cream which rounded off the meal, she wondered again where the fiancée was. Perhaps she would come that afternoon, or Lauris might go and fetch her from wherever she lived. He certainly went out after lunch, taking the car, with the casual remark that he would be back after tea. The boys saw him off and then declared their intention of going for a good long walk, leaving her and her hostess sitting opposite each other before the fire.

'I shall take you round the castle,' said Mevrouw van der Wagema, 'but there is no hurry. It has been in the family for a very long time and Lauris is very devoted to it.'

'I wonder why he lives in London,' ventured Julia, hoping it didn't sound rude.

'Well, my dear, his godfather was English and a doctor too, as was his father. And of course he went to Cambridge and took an English degree as well as degrees here. He is a little of both countries, and I am

appy that it is so. Of course, eventually, he will come
ere to live but at present he is content—or will be
hen he marries.'

'I—I expected to see his fiancée,' said Julia.

Mevrouw van der Wagema's handsome features
ecame as smooth and bland as her son's when he
anted to hide something. 'Oh, Lauris will make sure
that, my dear.'

'She sounds very nice.'

'She is—charming and so right for him—exactly
hat I would wish in a daughter-in-law. I do not very
uch care for the very young girls—you are thirty I
elieve?'

Julia said rather touchily. 'Yes, getting long in the
oth.'

'I would have said that you were at the height of
ur good looks, Julia. Also you do not look your age.
auris is a good deal older than you,' she added
uickly, 'and his fiancée.' Julia glanced at her; she
uld have sworn that her companion was amused
out something.

They had tea and little cakes around the fire later,
d then the boys came in, hungry as always and were
nt away to have a more substantial meal in what
sed to be the schoolroom when the professor and his
sters had been children. 'You shall see it presently,'
id Mevrouw van der Wagema, 'the grandchildren
e it whenever they come to stay.'

It was dark by the time the professor returned but
ere was no one with him. He made no mention of
here he had been, but sat and talked for a few
inutes before his mother observed that it was time
e changed her dress for the evening, a hint which
lia took willingly enough. She desperately wanted to

stay with Lauris, but common sense warned her not to

She was glad she had brought the green dress when she went downstairs. The professor had changed into a dark grey suit and a beautiful silk tie and his mother was in black velvet. The boys had spruced up too undoubtedly thinking it worth while in anticipation of the meal they hoped to enjoy.

They enjoyed lobster soup, roast duck, a delicious salad on the side and syllabub with lashings of cream and they drank champagne. The boys were allowed only a little of it, of course, but Julia, after two glasses felt that life wasn't so bad after all.

The evening was passed pleasantly, with the boys and Julia playing Scrabble on the rent table and the professor and his mother sitting at the other end of the room, talking quietly. Nicky, seeing Julia glance at them, explained kindly: 'They talk Fries together sometimes. They are now.'

No one stayed up late, it had been a long day and the plans for the morrow were copious. The boys went first, followed by Julia and her hostess. Lauris accompanied them to the foot of the stairs before turning away to go through a door opposite the drawing room.

'His study,' explained his mother as they reached the head of the stairs. 'Sleep well, my dear, it is delight to have you here.'

Contrary to her expectations Julia did sleep well, to wake while it was getting light and jump out of bed and peer down into the grounds below. There had been a frost and everything was covered in white. It looked tempting outside. No one would mind— indeed, no one need know—if she went outside and took a look around.

She showered and dressed in her slacks and her thickest woollen sweater, fastened her quilted jacket around her person, pulled the hood over her bright hair and crept around the gallery and down the stairs. There were faint sounds coming from behind a door which she supposed led to the kitchen, and a small lamp burned on the side table. She stood in the middle of the hall wondering if she dared open the great front door or find another smaller one. In a place this size there would be several, she guessed, and turned round to try doors she had not yet been through. She rotated slowly, deciding which one to try and then gave a gasp and came to a halt. Lauris was watching her from a narrow little door under the stairs.

'Good morning, Julia. I wonder why I was so sure that you would be up early? I've been waiting for you.'

'Me?' She was breathless. 'Oh, why?'

'Shall we go outside and walk around and I'll tell you.'

He held the little door open for her and she found herself in a small passage which wound round between white walls until it came to another small door which he opened. They stepped out into the pale light of early morning and she saw that they were at the back of the castle, with a long vista of lawns and flowers beds and trees at the far end. He took her arm and then, because she had forgotten her gloves, tucked her hand into his.

They had walked half way to the trees before she said carefully, 'What did you want to talk about?' and then suddenly exasperated, 'Lauris, I really can't go on like this and it's so unfair . . .'

'Unfair?' His voice was gently enquiring.

'Yes, to your fiancée—the girl you're going to

marry. I expected to meet her and I haven't and it just won't do. You said that she didn't mind but I know that I jolly well would . . .'

'Would you really? Would you be consumed with jealousy and tear me apart and probably throw something at me?'

'Yes—yes I would. She's too good to be true . . .'

'Oh, she's true enough.' They had reached the trees and she saw a little wooden summer house tucked cosily in the centre of them. He drew her inside and it was surprisingly warm out of the wind.

He said suddenly: 'Do you still love Longman?'

'Heavens, no, I thought I did, you know, but now I know that I didn't love him at all, not—not like . . .'

'Yes,' he prompted.

'Never mind. Just that I didn't know what loving someone was like.'

'Until you found that you loved me,' said the professor gently.

She raised her green eyes to his dark ones. 'That's unfair but quite true.' It was a relief to be able to say it. She felt quite light headed with the pleasure of getting it off her chest at last.

'Did it never strike you,' asked Lauris, 'that I might be in love with you?'

'No.' She thought briefly of his austere manner on the ward—hardly loverlike. 'And you can't be; you're going to be married.'

'So I am—to you, my darling girl.'

'But the other girl—your fiancée . . .'

'I never said that I had a fiancée,' he reminded her, 'I merely stated that I intended to get married. There is a difference if you think about it.'

'I'm in no state to think,' said Julia quite wildly,

and why didn't you tell me?'

He burst out laughing and caught her close. 'What? with Longman to start with and then you being suspicious each time I so much as looked at you? And so anxious not to poach on my fiancée's preserves. I began to despair that we would ever become friends, let alonE husband and wife.'

'There's no one else?'

He didn't bother to answer that but bent to kiss her very thoroughly. 'There's never been anyone else, my dearest. Nicky knows it and Mother knows it, your mother knows it. You are the one who's been hard to convince.' He kissed her again. 'You know I was on the point of proposing to you when you had that cold, but I thought you might not have liked it.'

'I most certainly wouldn't—I had a red nose and my hair needed washing.'

'I didn't mind. Oh, my darling, I said once that at the end of the day all we need is to love and be loved. I promise you that I will love you till the end of my days.'

She reached up and put her arms round his neck. And I promise you that you will always be loved. Oh, Lauris . . .'

She turned her face up to his and had it well kissed for her pains.

Here's how to get this special offer from Harlequin! As simple as 1...2...3!

1. Each month, save one Treasury Edition coupon from your favorite Romance or Presents novel.
2. In four months you'll have saved four Treasury Edition coupons (<u>only one coupon per month allowed</u>).
3. Then all you have to do is fill out and return the order form provided, along with the four Treasury Edition coupons required and $1.00 for postage and handling.

Mail to: Harlequin Reader Service

RT1-D-2

In the U.S.A.
2504 West Southern Ave.
Tempe, AZ 85282

In Canada
P.O. Box 2800, Postal Station A
5170 Yonge Street
Willowdale, Ont. M2N 6J3

Please send me my FREE copy of the Janet Dailey Treasury Edition. I have enclosed the four Treasury Edition coupons required and $1.00 for postage and handling along with this order form.

(Please Print)

NAME_____

ADDRESS_____

CITY_____

STATE/PROV._____ZIP/POSTAL CODE_____

SIGNATURE_____

This offer is limited to one order per household.

This special Janet Dailey offer expires January 1986.

SUPPLIES LIMITED

H·A·R·L·E·Q·U·I·N

FIRST·CLASS
Sweepstakes

OFFICIAL RULES

1. NO PURCHASE NECESSARY. To enter, complete the official entry/order form. Be sure to indicate whether or not you wish to take advantage of our subscription offer.

2. Entry blanks have been preselected for the prizes offered. Your response will be checked to see if you are a winner. In the event that these preselected responses are not claimed, a random drawing will be held from all entries received to award not less than $150,000 in prizes. This is in addition to any free, surprise or mystery gifts which might be offered. Versions of this sweepstakes with different prizes will appear in Preview Service Mailings by Harlequin Books and their affiliates. Winners selected will receive the prize offered in their sweepstakes brochure.

3. This promotion is being conducted under the supervision of Marden-Kane, an independent judging organization. By entering the sweepstakes, each entrant accepts and agrees to be bound by these rules and the decisions of the judges, which shall be final and binding. Odds of winning in the random drawing are dependent upon the total number of entries received. Taxes, if any, are the sole responsibility of the prize winners. Prizes are nontransferable. All entries must be received by August 31, 1986.

4. The following prizes will be awarded:

    (1) Grand Prize: Rolls-Royce™ *or* $100,000 Cash!
    (Rolls-Royce being offered by permission of
    Rolls-Royce Motors Inc.)

    (1) Second Prize: A trip for two to Paris for 7 days/6 nights. Trip includes air transportation on the Concorde, hotel accommodations...PLUS...$5,000 spending money!

    (1) Third Prize: A luxurious Mink Coat!

5. This offer is open to residents of the U.S. and Canada, 18 years or older, except employees of Harlequin Books, its affiliates, subsidiaries, Marden-Kane and all other agencies and persons connected with conducting this sweepstakes. All Federal, State and local laws apply. Void in the province of Quebec and wherever prohibited or restricted by law. Winners will be notified by mail and may be required to execute an affidavit of eligibility and release, which must be returned within 14 days after notification. Canadian winners will be required to answer a skill-testing question. Winners consent to the use of their name, photograph and/or likeness for advertising and publicity purposes in conjunction with this and similar promotions without additional compensation. One prize per family or household.

6. For a list of our most current prize winners, send a stamped, self-addressed envelope to: WINNERS LIST, c/o Marden-Kane, P.O. Box 10404, Long Island City, New York 11101